I'm a real ace at arguing with myself.

Take a subject like Tanner Cobb.

On the one hand, he stole.

On the other, he helped his little brother read and count.

Then again, he stole shoes in front of his little brother.

But he brought the shoes back and offered to make up for what he'd done.

My mind said, Don't trust him.

My instincts said, He might not be all bad.

Inconsistencies are a royal pain; the older you get, the more they multiply.

➤➤➤

Books by

JOAN BAUER

Backwater

Best Foot Forward

Hope Was Here

Rules of the Road

Squashed

Stand Tall

Sticks

Thwonk

JOAN BAUER

Best Foot Forward

speak
An Imprint of Penguin Group (USA) Inc.

01090 5643

SPEAK
Published by the Penguin Group
Penguin Group (USA) Inc., 345 Hudson Street, New York, New York 10014, U.S.A.
Penguin Group (Canada), 90 Eglinton Avenue East, Suite 700, Toronto,
Ontario, Canada M4P 2Y3 (a division of Pearson Penguin Canada Inc.)
Penguin Books Ltd, 80 Strand, London WC2R 0RL, England
Penguin Ireland, 25 St Stephen's Green, Dublin 2, Ireland (a division of Penguin Books Ltd)
Penguin Group (Australia), 250 Camberwell Road, Camberwell, Victoria 3124, Australia
(a division of Pearson Australia Group Pty Ltd)
Penguin Books India Pvt Ltd, 11 Community Centre, Panchsheel Park, New Delhi - 110 017, India
Penguin Group (NZ), Cnr Airborne and Rosedale Roads, Albany, Auckland 1310, New Zealand
(a division of Pearson New Zealand Ltd)
Penguin Books (South Africa) (Pty) Ltd, 24 Sturdee Avenue,
Rosebank, Johannesburg 2196, South Africa

Registered Offices: Penguin Books Ltd, 80 Strand, London WC2R 0RL, England

First published in the United States of America by G. P. Putnam's Sons,
a division of Penguin Young Readers Group, 2005
Published by Speak, an imprint of Penguin Group (USA) Inc., 2006

10 9 8 7 6 5 4 3 2 1

THE LIBRARY OF CONGRESS HAS CATALOGED THE G. P. PUTNAM'S SONS EDITION AS FOLLOWS:
Bauer, Joan, date. Best foot forward / Joan Bauer. p. cm.
Summary: Between school and Al-Anon meetings, Jenna helps Mrs. Gladstone cope with
escalating problems that result from the merger of Gladstone Shoes with Shoe Warehouse
Corporation, while managing a new employee with a shoplifting record.
[1. Stores, Retail—Fiction. 2. Business ethics—Fiction. 3. Shoplifting—Fiction.
4. Old age—Fiction. 5. Family problems—Fiction.] I. Title.
PZ7.B32615Bes 2005   [Fic]—dc22
2005001473 ISBN 0-399-23474-8 (hc)

Speak ISBN 0-14-240690-2

Printed in the United States of America

For *Jean*,
who always puts her best foot forward

And for *Steven*,
who never gives up

With deepest thanks to my editor,
Nancy Paulsen,
for her wisdom, perseverance, encouragement,
and tireless good cheer

My love and gratitude to friends
Rita, Laura, JoAnn, Chris, Jo Ellen, and Teri;
to my husband, Evan,
my sister, Karen, and my mom—
all remarkable sources of strength to me.

I am indebted to Willie McLean,
who shared his heart,
and to Ken Thrall, a man of true sole.

Best Foot Forward

Chapter 1

>>>>>>>>>>>>>>>>>>>>>>>>>>>>>>>>>>>>>>>

"Feet," said Dr. Suzanne Rodriguez over the phone, "are the most abused parts of the body."

I held my cell phone, wiggled my toes, and wrote that down.

"People don't understand how much better their lives could be if they took care of their feet."

I wrote, *Better Living Through Foot Care.* I was doing this interview in my parked car. Dr. Rodriguez was the fourth foot doctor I'd interviewed this week. It was all part of the new push at Gladstone Shoes, where I worked, to eclipse every other shoe company in the galaxy.

"Think, Jenna," my boss, Mrs. Gladstone, had said, "how splendid it would be if Gladstone's hired a podiatrist to train the sales force.

"Call all the local foot doctors," she had directed. "See which ones you like; we'll comprise a list and pick the best."

Mrs. Gladstone was a big idea person, which meant she didn't always think about reality. Chicago has scores of podiatrists.

"I'm a teenager," I'd mentioned. "I don't know how to do this."

"You'll learn," she had said. "Everyone likes to talk about what they do. Ask them how they feel about their job. Ask them where they think podiatric medicine is going. Ask them to tell you their hopes and dreams."

Dr. Rodriguez was going on and on about how, when she was a young girl, she hated her large feet and they were a source of embarrassment to her, and that was when she knew that she wanted to help others with foot shame lead lives of freedom and comfort. When you ask foot doctors about their hopes and dreams, prepare to plunge deep.

Other cars were pulling into the parking lot. My meeting was about to start.

I thanked Dr. Rodriguez, jumped out, and lovingly locked the door. My new car was glistening red and cool in the early morning light. People talk about light dancing off a lake in summer or sunshine pouring through a kitchen window, but there's a true beauty to light beaming off the hood of a recently washed red car that is absolutely yours.

I rushed across the parking lot, past the little peace garden with the stone bench that I was going to sit on if I ever had time to relax. I headed through the back door and climbed the long staircase.

"Hi, I'm Jenna," I said to the group seated around the oval table. "My dad's an alcoholic."

"Hi, Jenna," twenty voices said back.

I sat up straight and tried to look brave. This was the second meeting of Al-Anon I'd attended since I got back from Texas this summer. Al-Anon is a recovery group for people who have alcoholics in their lives. At the meeting last week I didn't say anything; now I was getting ready to spill my guts.

I gripped the table in the St. Francis room of the Holy Name Catholic Church where these meetings took place—it was old and scratched; initials were carved into the wood. I looked at the painting of St. Francis on the wall. He was standing in a forest in a white robe, arms out, surrounded by adoring woodland animals. He looked like a Disney character in a happy glade. I thought there should be another picture in this room, given what we were all dealing with. St. Francis could at least look like he had a headache.

"Something happened with my dad," I said. The fan blew a strong breeze across the room. This group knew all about things happening with fathers. Suddenly I felt like crying. I kept thinking about how Dad was driving drunk, how I was in the car and had to stop him. "The thing is, I had to turn my dad in to the police. I know if I hadn't done it he would have kept hurting himself or someone or me. I *know* that. I'm just trying to live with it because it's on his record forever now and I think he hates me." I didn't want to cry, so I focused on the two squirrels at St. Francis's feet, looking mellow. Why shouldn't they be mellow? There are no alcohol issues in the forest. Of course there are predators, fires. I guess it's always something.

I said, "I want to stay strong because I've got a good job and a lot of people are counting on me. So I'm trying to remember all the stuff I know about the disease and how it's not about me, but I keep having these nightmares of him in jail and how it's my fault. I couldn't seem to deal with all this myself. So"—I took a huge breath—"I came here."

I didn't look at the faces, just heard the words that came back to me.

"Thanks for sharing that, Jenna."

"You're brave to have done that, Jenna."

"You probably helped him."

"It's not your fault."

Not my fault . . .

Not my fault . . .

I wanted to carve that into the table, carve it on my heart and mind so I wouldn't forget.

Not my fault.

A fly buzzed across the table like a jet fighter going in low across a runway. Ron, our group leader, batted it away. "Setting boundaries," he said. "Let's talk about that."

"The healthier we are," said someone, "the more we need them."

"And have to fight for them," a woman offered as the fly dive-bombed her arm.

"Weekends are the worst," said a girl, Deenie. "My dad just checks out. He drinks until he can't walk and then he sits down and drinks until he can't talk. We just live around him; no one mentions it. He's there, but he's not."

I sat at the table, listening to the stories. It felt good to know

I wasn't alone. My dad doesn't live with us anymore; I was eight when Mom kicked him out.

This fly had a death wish. It landed on Ron's nose and buzzed off to the wall. Ron rolled up the "12 Steps of Al-Anon" sheet; the twelve steps are principles for life, guidelines for getting stronger. Ron stood on his chair, and with one sure blow nailed it.

"Sometimes," said Ron, "you have to absolutely, completely, with all the strength you've got, say stop."

It was a major victory for boundary setting.

We all laughed. It was good to be back.

After Ron closed the meeting, we bowed our heads and said the Serenity Prayer: "God grant me the serenity to accept the things I cannot change, the courage to change the things I can, and the wisdom to know the difference."

A short girl sitting at the end of the table was crying. Everybody's got a big story here. Ron went over to her. I wanted to stay, but I'd be late for work if I did. School was starting in three weeks; I had so much to do at the shoe store before the big door of junior year slammed shut around me.

Leave your burdens at the table. That's what Jocelyn, my first Al-Anon group leader, used to say. I never quite knew how to do that back then. But I've changed so much since those days. I touched the table, lifted the hurt off my back, and plopped the mess down.

The table didn't crack, which I took as an excellent sign.

"Bye," I said to the group.

"Bye, Jenna."

I ran out to my car, got in, and breathed deep. Mr. Bovier, my Driver's Ed teacher, was always warning our class not to drive when we're emotional—*only* well adjusted, unemotional people should ever drive, he insisted. Mr. Bovier was completely unemotional except when you'd forget to signal a turn across oncoming traffic.

I started my car; it purred hello. I'd bought it with my own hard-earned money, bought it as soon as I got back from Texas this summer to celebrate my newfound maturity and the changes I was making in my life. I took a few cleansing breaths.

I checked my rearview mirror, looked behind me, and pulled out of the Holy Name parking lot as unemotionally as a teenager could manage.

Chapter 2

>>>>>>>>>>>>>>>>>>>>>>>>>>>>>>>>>>>>>>

"Is it okay to play with the squirrels?"

The little boy stood in the children's shoe section by the huge tree I'd made. Big green leaves made out of construction paper hung from the branches.

"Sure," I said. "There's a whole squirrel family there—a father, a mother, a—"

"There's *no* father." He stood on his toes to get the animals down. "And the mother's sleeping." He threw a squirrel on the floor and lifted the others out. "This is the grandmother."

I shook hands with the grandmother squirrel. "How are you, Grandma?"

"She's doing okay, except she has to work too hard."

I smiled. "Gathering nuts takes a lot out of you."

He nodded seriously.

Two businessmen walked in and marched to the men's oxfords. You have to have great range to work at Gladstone Shoes—I moved from forest family dynamics to assisting Corporate America.

"Gentlemen, can I help you?"

I didn't need to measure their feet. These guys knew. The older man held up a square-toed oxford. "Eleven medium."

"Same shoe," said the younger man, "in ten and a half."

It's a privilege to wait on decision makers. "Great shoes," I said and headed to the back, giving Murray Castlebaum, my other boss, a sympathetic look. Murray's customer wasn't sure about anything—she'd pick a shoe up, carry it around, then put it back in the wrong place. Murray kept asking her if he could help.

She shook her head. "I'm just looking."

In five minutes she'd rearranged half the store. We call it search and destroy in the shoe world.

I headed to the back room, jumped on the sliding ladder and got the shoes, raced back to the businessmen, slipped the oxfords on their feet. They stood in unison. The older man nodded. "Sold."

Poor Murray. Now his customer wanted help. She held up shoe after shoe. "Do you have this in brown?"

"Just black and camel," Murray told her. She put the shoes on the floor.

"Do you have this sandal in teal blue?"

"It doesn't come in any kind of blue."

"Does this come with a closed toe?"

Murray gripped a chair. *It's a sandal.*

"Well," she sighed, "I guess I'll have to go *someplace* else."

Would you *please?*

Murray rolled his eyes at me.

A teenage girl walked up to the little boy and told him he could play a few more minutes. She leaned down to him and whispered intently before going over to the stiletto heels. Don't, I wanted to tell her. You're young. Don't destroy your feet.

"I'm four and three-eighths," the little boy announced proudly to me. "I can write my name!"

"Wow," I said. "You're old."

Murray muttered that he was fifty-four and a half and getting older by the minute.

The little boy pointed to the tree leaves. Each kid got to write their name on a leaf. I gave him a paper leaf and a crayon.

A teenage guy came in. He had tan skin and short, curly hair and walked toward the athletic shoes. A long scar ran from just below his left eye to his jaw.

The guy kept glancing at me. He had intense, dark eyes. "What kind of shoes are those?" he asked Murray, pointing to a support walker with extra cushioning. He had a low, earthy voice.

"They're for women who are on their feet most of the day and need extra support."

"You got them in an eight?"

"What color?"

"How many colors you got?"

Murray said he'd check.

The little boy handed me his leaf with WEBSTER T. COBB on it.

"You can put that up anywhere on the tree, Webster."

Murray came back with an armful of shoe boxes. The teenage girl stepped in front of him and grabbed her stomach. "I feel sick," she moaned. "Can I please have some water?" She motioned to the boy weakly. "Webster, come here."

Webster's face clouded over. "She's okay."

"*Webster* . . . I think I'm going to faint."

"I'll get you water," I told the girl. I rushed in the back room and filled a paper cup.

Wait a minute—a red flag went up.

The girl, that nervous guy. Suddenly, everything felt wrong. I heard Murray scream, *"Come back with those!"*

I raced back to the floor, looked around, but the teenage guy was gone.

Murray has many gifts, but running is not one of them. He lurched out the door screaming, "Stop! Thief!" The girl marched over to Webster. She tried to take his hand.

"Webster, we're going!"

Murray walked back into the store with the security guard. Murray's eyes turned to slits as he looked at the girl.

"You know that boy who stole those shoes?"

The girl grabbed Webster's hand and yanked him toward her. I knew that shoplifters sometimes work in twos. One creates a disturbance while the other one grabs merchandise and runs out the door.

"Do you know him?"

"I don't know what you're talking about."

"You're a witness to a crime," Murray informed her. "You're going to have to wait until the police come."

"I'm leaving, mister!"

Webster started crying, pulling away from the girl.

Just then, Mrs. Gladstone came down from her office above the store. "What in God's name . . . ?"

"We had an incident," Murray said.

The girl was yanking Webster's hand, telling him to stop crying; Webster broke free and ran toward the tree. He was wheezing, trying to catch his breath. Mrs. Gladstone stared at the girl. "Is that child sick?"

"He has trouble breathing sometimes," she said. "Webster, come on. Use your inhaler."

Webster nodded pitifully—he had huge eyes. He stuck an inhaler in his mouth and took a gasping breath.

Mrs. Gladstone was not a large woman, but the strength of her presence made up for it. She walked over to Webster and bent down as much as she could. "My son had trouble breathing sometimes when he was your age. You're doing fine, just let yourself relax. It's going to be okay."

Her voice was so gentle. Webster closed his eyes and breathed more normally. Mrs. Gladstone's son is now a world-class business sleaze, a supreme shoe scorpion, and, unfortunately, the new head of this company.

She smiled. "I have a storybook that you might like to look at." She walked to the register and came back with *The Elves and the Shoemaker*. Webster plopped down on the floor, put the squirrels in his lap, and opened the book. He pointed to a word. "Shoe."

"That's right," Mrs. Gladstone said. "Shoe."

Webster scrunched up his face, pointed to more words. "Bed. Old. Night."

Mrs. Gladstone smiled. "Who taught you to read those words?"

"Tanner."

"Shut up!" the girl shouted.

Webster looked down.

"Who's Tanner?" Mrs. Gladstone asked him.

"Just a friend!" the girl insisted.

Webster shook his head. His dark, intense eyes seemed familiar.

"Was Tanner here at the store with you?" I asked.

"Yes." Webster turned the page as the girl groaned. He pointed to a word. "Go."

Murray faced the girl. "Who was the boy who stole the shoes? We're going to find out sooner or later."

The girl started crying. "He's our brother." Her cell phone began to ring.

"If that's Tanner," Mrs. Gladstone said, "tell him to come back with the shoes."

The girl answered, crying softly. ". . . Well, you get back here, that's what. 'Cause we're here and they won't let us go. . . . *I can't help it—Webster told 'em.* You'd better bring it all back!"

Chapter 3

>>

Tanner stormed through the door holding four shoe boxes, his square jaw clenched tight.

"Is that everything?" Murray demanded.

"Yeah," he snarled.

I dialed Mrs. Gladstone's extension. She'd gone upstairs to her office with Webster and the girl. "He's here," I told her.

· Mrs. Gladstone, Webster, and the girl came down looking like they'd become pals. Tanner glared at his sister. *"Thanks for nothing, Yaley."*

"What do you want me to do, Tanner, sit here and rot while you're—"

Mrs. Gladstone slammed her hand on the register counter. *"That's enough!"*

That shut them up for a minute. Tanner stood there like a caged animal. He stared at me and I stared back, even though he scared me. I walked to the register extra tall and I had height to pull from—I'm five-eleven.

The front door opened and an older woman walked in.

Yaley started crying when she saw her.

Webster said, "Hi, Grandma."

"Hi, sugar. You okay?"

Webster nodded as Mrs. Gladstone stepped forward. "You must be Mattie. I'm very glad you could come."

The grandmother looked straight at Mrs. Gladstone. "I want to thank you for calling me." She took Tanner by the elbow. Tanner muttered something. "Tanner Cobb, speak up directly and look this woman in the eye when you address her."

His whole body went stiff; he looked at Mrs. Gladstone with those electric eyes. "I'm sorry for what I did."

Mrs. Gladstone considered that. "Tanner, I have a feeling you've done this before."

"Once or twice . . . you know . . ."

"I wish I could be everywhere," Mattie interrupted, "but I can't. Still, these children are under my roof and they're my responsibility. I take that very seriously."

"It's a hard world out there for young people," Mrs. Gladstone offered.

"Amen, but these two are making it harder than it needs to be." She glared at Tanner and Yaley as Webster ran back to play with the tree.

Tanner forced a smile. "I could help out at the store to make up for what I did."

"I'll think about that, young man." Mrs. Gladstone had a strange look on her face. "Mattie, I'll call you and we can discuss this. For now, I'm not pressing charges."

Tanner and Yaley looked relieved.

I tried to get Mrs. Gladstone's eye—*We don't need a thief in the store.*

Webster walked up to me and held out two leaves he'd written on. One read TANNER, the other YALEY. He took me by the hand and we walked to the children's tree. He dragged the footstool over, stood on it, fastened the leaves on a higher branch, and stepped down, satisfied.

I hadn't quite envisioned the names of shoplifters on the tree. I said, "Boy, we've got a lot of names up there."

"We've got forty-three names."

"We do?"

Webster began to count the names out loud to show me. I bent down. "Who taught you to count like that, Webster?"

He looked across the room and smiled. "Tanner."

It was 6:00 P.M. I drove Mrs. Gladstone's old Cadillac through the Chicago traffic. The heat of the day hadn't lifted yet—typical for August in Chicago.

Deep snoring rose from the backseat; Mrs. Gladstone's head bobbed up and down in fitful sleep. We'd spent six weeks on the road together driving from Chicago down to Texas. We got to know each other pretty well. I know her favorite food (chili with hot peppers); I know her greatest strength (not losing control); I've seen the full panorama of her personality (stern, sterner, and run for your life). She's always taken a tough stand on shoplifters until now.

The goal of the trip was to get to Dallas for Gladstone Shoes' annual stockholders meeting so that Mrs. Gladstone could retire as president of the company and hand the reins of leadership over to her son. All told, she had a thirty-minute retirement before she got appointed Director of Quality Control for the newly merged shoe empire. Gladstone's was bought by the Shoe Warehouse Corporation. Right now, everyone was trying to get used to all the changes.

Mrs. Gladstone rustled in the backseat. I could hear her straighten up, which wasn't easy with her bad hip.

I glanced in the rearview mirror. "Are you okay back there?"

"I'm fine, I'm fine."

A meteor could fall splat into Lake Michigan, causing rampaging floods, and she'd still say she was fine.

"Do you want me to call the doctor's office tomorrow and schedule your surgery?"

"I do not." Hip replacement surgery wasn't high on her to-do list, even though earlier this summer she had to be in a wheelchair because of the pain. She was an ace at changing the subject, too.

"Yaley and I had quite a talk," she offered. "That girl is smart and has too much on her shoulders for a fourteen-year-old."

I could relate, but I didn't go around ripping people off.

"She told me her father is in prison and her mother is a drug addict."

Okay, so maybe she outweighed me on the bad parent scale.

"Can you imagine having a parent in jail, Jenna?"

Yes, actually. "It's tough, I'm sure," I said, and turned left onto North Avenue. "Do you know what her father's in jail for?"

"I didn't ask. She said her brother stole the shoes for their grandmother's birthday."

I looked at her determined old face in the rearview mirror. "Do you believe her?"

"Yes, for the most part I do." She looked out the window. "Let me tell you something about me, Jenna. The longer I'm alive, the more I'm interested in how people learn from their mistakes, not in the fact that they make them."

But we *don't know* if they've learned from their mistakes, do we?

I stopped in front of Mrs. Gladstone's three-story brownstone and walked her to the steps, where Maria, her housekeeper, took over. They headed slowly up the stairs. I pressed the button that lifted the garage door and backed my red car onto the street. I always parked it here, then drove Mrs. Gladstone to work and back in her car. I steered the Cadillac into the garage.

I sat there in this car that had changed my life. For the first time ever, I hoped my English teacher would ask us to write an essay on What I Did on My Summer Vacation. I'd let the words and the memories spill out about Mrs. Gladstone's all-out grit, and how hanging out with old people really has its moments. It pays well, too. I'd write about meeting Harry Bender and how knowing him for just a week changed my life.

Changing lives was Harry's specialty. He could have changed so many more, too, if he hadn't gotten killed.

I walked onto the street, pushed the garage door button; the door creaked down. I'll tell you what the world needs—a button to push to turn back the time.

I climbed into my red car and took the long way home.

Chapter 4

▸▸▸▸▸▸▸▸▸▸▸▸▸▸▸▸▸▸▸▸▸▸▸▸▸▸▸▸▸▸▸▸▸▸▸▸▸▸

How to Get Flat Abs, a Firm Butt, and Be Lean All Over.

That was on the cover of the magazine my little sister, Faith, was reading.

I gazed at my stomach that had never been flat; considered my behind that I never had to look at, so whether it was firm wasn't a consuming issue for me. I'd lost thirteen pounds this summer, but lean was a long way off.

"Hi." I put my briefcase down heavily. "How are you doing?"

"Look, Jenna, I need your help."

Faith stood before me in a white skirt with knee-high boots and a hot pink tank top. Faith had one goal—to be a world-famous model. She shoved a paper at me. "I've got to practice for my modeling class, so you shout these directions to me, and I'm supposed to change expressions."

Faith changed expressions a hundred times a day; I didn't see why she needed prompts. She started walking across the room in long strides, one hand on her hip, not blinking. I looked at the sheet and called out, "Casual and free."

She stomped her foot. *"That's what I'm doing now!"*

"Okay, sorry! Be challenging. . . ."

Faith shook her head, her cheekbones got higher, her eyes looked straight ahead. She took harder steps. Not bad.

"Happy and demure . . ."

A little smile played across her face; her eyes brightened; her steps got smaller; she swung her purse as she walked.

"Exciting," I said.

"I'm not good at this one."

"Well, try."

She half bit her lip, raised her eyebrows in anticipation.

"More excitement," I shouted. "Make me thrilled!"

She stopped in her tracks. "You are so bossy, Jenna!"

"You asked me to help!"

"Not like that!"

She flounced out. Models know how to make a big exit.

I went to the kitchen; put water on to boil.

I looked at the wall calendar: TODAY IS AUGUST 21.

I stared at the date; it hadn't registered until now.

I looked up to see Faith standing there by the kitchen door. She shook out her hair. "Happy birthday, Daddy."

"I forgot," I said.

We always make a big deal out of birthdays in our family, but it's hard to celebrate someone when you never know quite where they are. Last year I got a cake and Faith and I sang "Happy Birthday" to an empty chair. It was so depressing—a colossal waste of devil's food and fudge frosting.

20

She plopped down on a stool. "What do you think he's doing? You think he's drunk by now?" she asked like a little kid.

I checked my watch—8:00 P.M. "Probably."

My pasta boiled over. I poured the linguini into a colander, felt the hot steam rise against my face, added peppers, garlic, grated fresh cheese over it, let that melt just a moment, divided it into two bowls, and pushed one toward her.

I took a wooden spoon and bonged a pan hanging from the pot rack overhead. "Happy birthday, Dad, wherever you are."

Faith lit the tea candles in the blue glass bowl.

"I hate Dad," she said softly, eating her pasta.

I knew she loved him, too. We'd talked about this a lot—you can hate what someone does, but still love the person.

It's not the easiest concept to embrace. It's right up there with not making excuses for bad behavior. I spent a lot of years making excuses for Dad.

Faith twisted a tendril of her hair. "What would you say if Dad walked in here right now?"

I ate some pasta. "I'd ask him how he got the key."

She elbowed me. *"Seriously."*

"I don't know, Faith. The last time I saw him, it didn't go too well."

She twisted that curl tighter. "At least you saw him."

Faith was throwing little pieces of paper into the tea light flames and watching them burn up.

"Look, Faith, do you want to come to an Al-Anon meeting with me? They can really help to—"

"Mom says I don't need to go."

"What do *you* say?"

She shrugged.

The glow of the candles flickered through the leaded blue glass, casting an upward light on the wall calendar.

TODAY IS AUGUST 21.

Do you know where your father is?

I sat at the computer, looked at the screen.

> **Dear Dad,**
>
> I lost someone I loved this summer and that's why I'm writing to you—I don't want to lose you, too. His name was Harry. I didn't know him very long. He was a salesman like you. I worked with him when I went to Texas. He became my friend for a few weeks and then he got killed by a drunk driver. He used to have trouble with drinking himself, but he quit and was helping other people do the same. He said we don't know how much longer we'll have on this earth, so we'd better let people know we love them now.
>
> I never let him know I loved him, Dad. But I want you to know that I love you. I know that your drinking has brought you and me a lot of pain and misunderstanding. I know that you see it differently than I do, but I love you and that is real. I want you

to know that despite what happened, I carry you
with me in my heart.

I hope that if you read this letter you won't ever
doubt that.

Happy Birthday.

Jenna

Mom came in late from her date, looking happy. With her
new boyfriend and her crazy schedule at the hospital, we
didn't get to see each other much. "Hi, stranger. How are you?"

"Fine," I said, turning off the computer.

She sat on the couch, kicked off her shoes, and looked at me
hopefully. I give the best foot rub of anyone in the family.
Mom starts off strong, but she gives up after only a minute. I
rubbed the soft section of the balls of her feet in a circular mo-
tion, so as not to do further injury. I rubbed and massaged the
arches, touching on all the pressure points.

You can't quit too soon when you're dealing with feet.
You've got to stay the course. I kicked off my shoes because
my blister was hurting.

I'm a real ace at handling pain, emotional and otherwise.

Chapter 5

≻≻≻≻≻≻≻≻≻≻≻≻≻≻≻≻≻≻≻≻≻≻≻≻≻≻≻≻≻≻

I was driving Mrs. Gladstone to work and she was on the phone already, fighting back the enemies of excellence who just want to cut corners here and there and think nobody will notice. "Well, the real problem," she was saying, "is that everyone has a different definition of quality. We have to get one definition and work toward that." She hung up and sighed. She's been sighing a lot since we got back from Texas.

She's been shouting a lot, too. As Director of Quality Control for the Shoe Warehouse Corporation, Mrs. Gladstone gets paid to find problems and shout about them until they're fixed. Finding problems around here isn't hard since Gladstone's merged with the Shoe Warehouse this summer. The early bonding phase hasn't been pretty.

To begin with, there was the big debate about how to answer the phone. Do we say, "Hello, Gladstone Shoes," or, "Hello, Gladstone Shoes/Shoe Warehouse," or just, "Hello, we're confused." Then there was the fear factor—will everyone keep their jobs? Followed by the financial factor—will salaries go up, down, or stay the same? And then there was the fudge factor—how truthful were the recent reports on how well our shoes were selling?

Mrs. Gladstone was particularly interested in that. She rustled in the backseat. "Yes, Riley. . . . I want *all* the numbers you have for returns per store by brand. I want all the numbers from the factories as well. We can't find out how to make things better until we see where we are. . . . No, I need it much sooner than that. . . . Next week."

Mrs. Gladstone was on fire to make things better, but not everyone appreciates the heat. Ken Woldman, the Chief Executive Officer of the Shoe Warehouse Corporation, keeps telling her to slow down, change takes time, that he's fine with cutting a few corners here and there. Then there's Elden Gladstone, her ungrateful son, who keeps telling her how the business has changed and people care more about price than quality. Murray calls Elden "General Manager in Charge of Always Doing the Wrong Thing." He's very good at his job, too, at least how Murray defines it. Whenever Mrs. Gladstone has a phone call with Elden, she swallows an extra dose of pain medication because the sheer frustration of having a son like that starts her bad hip to throbbing.

I drove down Wells Street. I hated to admit this, but my shoes were hurting. I've sold shoes for over a year and I pride myself on knowing how to get a proper fit. These were a new pair, too—Gladstone's best-selling brand that bears our exclusive label:

We make them in our factory in Bangor, Maine. Mrs. Gladstone told me there wasn't a better shoe factory anywhere. "From the factory workers to the designers," she said, "every step underscores quality." People don't realize that over 160 steps go into making a good pair of shoes. Why these hurt was a mystery. I had the right amount of room in the toe, the cut wasn't close to my ankles. I wondered if I'd changed so much this summer that my feet changed shape to keep up with the rest of me.

When we got to the store, Murray was in a snit about the memo that had come from Ken Woldman:

> **One of the Shoe Warehouse's most beloved
> symbols, our bell, will be sent to all Gladstone
> stores. Please ring the bell with pride every time
> a customer buys two pairs of shoes or more.
> This is our way of letting our customers know
> we appreciate them.**

"I don't ring bells," Murray said. "It's in my contract."

Mrs. Gladstone looked at the memo and sighed. "Let's wait till the bell arrives and then decide."

"And this notice here," Murray said shrilly, "says all Gladstone stores will be having daily specials on different brands. *Daily?* What are we running—a grocery store?"

Mrs. Gladstone's cheek twitched. "I'll talk to Ken."

Murray held the top of his stomach, which meant his diverticulitis was acting up.

Throughout the day Mrs. Gladstone kept coming out of her office, muttering disturbing things.

"I think we could use a strong pair of arms around here."

"The storeroom could certainly use a big cleaning."

Then she'd turn on her heel, go back into her office, shut the door, and start shouting at someone on the phone.

"You don't think she's going to let that Tanner guy come work here, do you, Murray?"

"Madeline gets these soft spots for people down on their luck."

I groaned.

"I remember when you came in, kid. You needed work, you know, but you also needed *work*. I say that with respect for what you've done."

"Was I that bad?"

"You had the guts to walk in and ask for a job, you wanted to work, but like anything new, it took you a while to get your footing." Murray chuckled at the shoe joke. "But what you had is what everybody needs to succeed—you had heart."

"Thanks, Murray."

"I took a chance on you, kid." I hadn't realized I was such a big risk. "And you didn't let me down. You know why?"

"Because I have heart?"

"Because you were desperate."

"I was?"

27

He leaned against the wall next to the poster of our new Gladstone leather walking sandal that basically turned a common man into a mountain goat for just $79.95. "See, desperation is the driving force in finding work. You've got to know you want work, you've got to know you need it. And when you've figured that out, you've got to take the steps and take the chances to make it happen. A desperate person is a hungry person. You follow me?"

I thought back to that time. I guess I was desperate for something to happen to me. I needed something that wasn't just for kids—I needed to make money, be out of the house, learn something entirely new.

"I've been managing shoe people for twenty-three years," Murray said, "and there's two things I look for."

I smiled. "Heart and desperation."

"No, kid."

This was like one of those multiple-choice literature tests where you wondered if the teacher bothered to read the book.

"I look for character and adaptability."

"Okay..."

"See, character always comes through and I don't want anybody in here I can't trust near the public's feet or the cash register. I don't want anybody in here who's going to lie about shoes just to make a sale. That'll put us out of business like that. I look for adaptability because we're dealing with the whole of humanity, and you've got to be flexible because people are strange and feet are complicated." Murray got a faraway look in his eye. "It's not like selling ice cream, where people stop by for a cheap treat—whether they get strawberry or chocolate chip isn't going to touch a life. But with a shoe, kid, we're touching a person in a personal way. We hold their feet in our hands. Only a person of character and adaptability sees that as a calling."

I gulped. "Right."

Just then, Mrs. Gladstone came onto the floor, triumphant. "I think Tanner could be of use to us and that we could be of use to him."

"I can clean up the back room this week, ma'am. I won't sleep until it's done, I swear."

"I've already called his grandmother. He'll start tomorrow."

"Madeline, be careful. You've got a soft spot that could use some hardening," Murray cautioned.

"You're probably right." Her steel gray eyes looked tired. "My father always told me that in this world we're going to make a truckload of mistakes, but the best mistake we can ever make is to err on the side of mercy."

Murray put a stack of twenties in the register and locked the drawer. "My father told me the same thing, but he also said to watch your back."

I was thinking about the wisdom of fathers. I wished my dad had given me memorable advice on handling difficult situations. Instead he told me endless times, "When you're making a martini, you've got to be careful not to bruise the gin." He'd take out his special martini stirrer and gently stir the gin and vermouth to demonstrate. This doesn't have far-reaching applications when you're feeling threatened. I think Dad was easier on the gin than he ever was on me, Mom, Faith, or himself.

Right versus wrong collided in my brain. Thanks to that semester of debate, I'm a real ace at arguing with myself. Take a subject like Tanner Cobb.

On the one hand, he stole.

On the other, he helped his little brother read and count.

Then again, he stole shoes in front of Webster.

But, he brought the shoes back and offered to make up for what he'd done.

My mind said, Don't trust him.

My instincts said, He might not be all bad.

Inconsistencies are a royal pain; the older you get, the more they multiply.

Like blisters. My skin was being ripped to shreds. At lunch, I limped pitifully to the Thai Garden Restaurant to have lunch with my best friend, Opal.

"It came," she said miserably.

"How bad is it?"

She shook her head. "Worse than I could have imagined."

Opal was going to be a bridesmaid at her cousin's wedding. She held up a picture of the bridesmaid's dress—a poufy pink and blue atrocity with puffed sleeves, ruffles, and an enormously full skirt covered with bows. It came with a straw hat.

"I'll look like Little Bo-Peep on steroids," she wailed. "What kind of shoes do you wear with something like this?"

I bit my lip. "Wooden?"

"I give this marriage six months, tops." She flopped in the chair.

She couldn't see the humor now, but she would when it was over. I raised my chicken satay spear. Opal and I try to find the funny side of life's dark moments. We can both takes ourselves pretty seriously. After my father showed up drunk on Parents' Night a few years ago, Opal said it sure took the pressure off my plummeting grade in Spanish. When Opal was playing so badly at her piano recital and her father stood up in the audience and bellowed, "That's enough!" I said, "Well, at least you didn't have to play the whole song through. You always hated that song."

I told her about Tanner coming to work at the store. "Should I be worried?" I asked.

Her face grew grim. "He sounds scary *and* hot, Jenna, which isn't the best combination. My father always tells me that facing fears makes us stronger. I'm not sure how much stronger you need to get."

Chapter 6

▶▶▶▶▶▶▶▶▶▶▶▶▶▶▶▶▶▶▶▶▶▶▶▶▶▶▶▶▶▶▶▶▶

Tanner Cobb was wearing khakis and scuffed brown shoes with a blue shirt—no belt. His hair was slicked back, which made his black eyes seem even more intense. It was hard for me to look at him straight on because there was something in him, energy, maybe, that just jumped out at you. I suppose Opal would consider him dangerously cute. My grandmother, who'd been married three times and had boyfriends up till she went into the nursing home, always told me, "If you smell danger on a man, run."

Tanner was studying the shoes we had displayed, taking everything in. Mrs. Gladstone was telling him how a shoe store isn't about individuals, it's about a community of people working together to serve the customers. "Jenna has been with us for over a year and she has contributed in remarkable ways to the success of the business."

That felt good. I stood tall.

"And Murray Castlebaum has seen it all," Mrs. Gladstone offered.

"Everything," Murray said threateningly. As threatening as a skinny guy with three strands of hair and a chicken neck can get.

"Tanner," said Mrs. Gladstone, "I respect the fact that you came here today. I want you to understand that what you'll be doing in the stockroom is still part of making this business run."

He nodded, a bit surprised. I don't think he was expecting to work back there.

"Jenna will show you the stockroom."

I glared at Mrs. Gladstone. *I don't want to go in the back with him.*

"Murray, on second thought, why don't you show Tanner?"

Murray looked Tanner in the eyes, searching, probably for heart, desperation, character, and adaptability. "We've got a lot of boxes."

Tanner slumped. "I'm strong."

"They got to be cut up just right or Nolan the recycling guy has a conniption. He lives and dies by whether the twine is tied perfect."

"I know how to do it."

Not too humble, this guy.

Murray reached for the sole. "Okay, kid, you're about to enter the exciting shoe world from the ground floor up, which is where I started."

Tanner put his hands in his pockets; Murray lifted his like an actor going into a long speech.

"Most people walk into a shoe store and don't think about

anything except getting shod, but in the walls of this place are hidden the voices of those who have come before." Tanner's eyes glazed over, but he snapped to when Murray pointed to the security camera. "Just so you know, we've got those everywhere."

Mrs. Gladstone cleared her throat. *Everywhere* was a nice concept to introduce, even though we only had one camera.

Tanner swaggered up to the camera and waved. "Hey, Mama." He grinned like he was God's gift to retail.

I started to laugh, caught myself.

Murray took Tanner in the back. Mrs. Gladstone smiled. "That was an auspicious start, I'd say."

I didn't say anything because I couldn't remember what *auspicious* meant. I dug back through vocab lessons—it either meant things went pretty well or the whole situation smelled suspicious.

I walked upstairs to my desk that was outside Mrs. Gladstone's office. Her big office was at corporate headquarters in Dallas, Texas, but this year she'd been spending most of her time in Chicago, so much so that she turned the second floor above the store into decent office space. Decent for her, that is.

As desks go, mine wasn't much—a scratched steel monster shoved against the wall. I'd been reading articles in magazines about how to turn a cramped, windowless corner into something that shouts home. I moved the fake ficus tree to the side, dusted my plastic foot model, adjusted the fringed pillow my grandma made for me when she could still sew. A little better, but not quite home.

I was wading through Mrs. Gladstone's report, *The History of Gladstone Shoes and Our Insistence on Quality No Matter What.* There aren't too many surprises when you have a title like that—it's like *The Texas Chainsaw Massacre.* You know the gist before you've even met the characters. As business stories go, it was a good one—how Mrs. Gladstone and her husband, Floyd, started the company right after World War II with a loan from the GI Bill; how they built it, shoe by shoe, with heart and quality. When Floyd died suddenly, Mrs. Gladstone took over. "I didn't have his business experience," she wrote, "but I knew his heart, so I started there."

I liked the thought of one person's heart being so strong, it could be a foundation to build on. My grandmother's heart was like that; Harry Bender's heart was always open to the needs of others. In different ways, they'd both known such hard times, but it seemed to make their hearts bigger, not smaller.

"I did the boxes."

Tanner Cobb stood by my desk. I only jumped a little. He couldn't have finished that job already. It would have taken me all day.

"What's next?" he asked.

Mrs. Gladstone shouted from her office, "I think you deserve a break. Jenna, show Tanner where we keep the refrigerator."

I tried to signal how profoundly bad an idea this was, but her phone rang and she was off. "Yes, I *know* we can save money by using cheaper leather, but we're not going to do that on the Gladstone brands. Ken Woldman and I have already discussed this."

I gulped. "Let's go look and see what you did first, Tanner." And pray that I'm not making the mistake of my life.

We headed to the back room. I wondered how Tanner would take criticism. That's one of the signs of maturity. You can't be in business without learning to take it on the chin.

I opened the storeroom door and gasped.

There were the boxes, all of them cut, tied, perfectly stacked. The knife was lying on a table, which I was glad to see. I scanned it for signs of blood—it was clean.

Okay, I was impressed. "You did a great job, Tanner. Thanks."

He shrugged, half smiled. "So where's the food?"

Tanner had just guzzled three bottles of apple juice and was eating his second banana. He looked around the stockroom, piled floor to ceiling with shoe boxes. Was he trying to figure out how to steal them?

"Got a lot of shoes here," he said.

"Well, yeah, it's a shoe store."

He half laughed like the joke was on me. "So when am I gonna sell shoes?"

"I don't know about that, Tanner. You just got here."

"I can do it."

"Everyone thinks selling shoes is easy; it's *not*."

"You gotta read people. Right?"

"Right."

"So, I read people." He leaned toward me, too close. "I know what they want."

I said, "That'll only help you if you're right."

He laughed. "I read *you*."

I don't like this.

"And you don't like me. You think I'm trouble."

I looked at him—his dark eyes laughed at me. "I don't like people who steal."

He pointed a finger at me. "See, I was right."

"And you," I said, "like to make people feel uncomfortable."

"Not me."

"Sure you do. You can't sell shoes like that."

That made him think. "So how do you sell 'em?"

I'm clicking through Murray's list—heart first, desperation, which might be a bad concept to introduce; humility, adaptability. "You go out there and want to do the best by people."

"What do you mean?"

"You want to really help them, Tanner. Make them comfortable, not just sell them something they don't need."

Just then his phone rang. He snapped it off his belt. "Yeah? . . . Oh, hi, Baby. I can't talk now. . . . Oh, yeah I do. . . ." He smiled, his voice got softer. "Now, Baby, you know I do. . . ." He half laughed, hung up. "She's used to me being more available."

"Break's over!" I stood to full height. He got up, left the empty glass bottles on the floor with the banana peels.

"Tanner, those get washed out and put into the blue bin. The banana peels go into the trash." I sounded pretty bossy. "Sorry, I don't mean to sound like your mother."

He scooped up the peels, slam-dunked them in the trash. "My mother don't talk to me much."

Chapter 7

>>>>>>>>>>>>>>>>>>>>>>>>>>>>>>>

The official word came down from Ken Woldman on daily
store specials.

They get customers in the store.

Every store will participate.

The window sales signs came that afternoon.

TODAY ONLY	TODAY ONLY
Ballet Flats **15% OFF**	*Ladies Dress Pumps* **20% OFF**
TODAY ONLY	TODAY ONLY
Cap-Toed Oxfords **20% OFF**	*Summer Sandals* **15% OFF**

But which TODAY ONLY special was for today?

We hadn't been told that newspaper ads and coupons had
been distributed.

We didn't have enough shoes to meet customer demand.

Then we'd forget to take the signs down in the windows and people would expect yesterday's specials today.

"I can't remember what's on sale anymore," Murray shouted, checking the weekly sheet. He'd ask Tanner to organize the shoes for the daily specials. But that's hard to do when you're not sure what's on sale. Tanner lugged out the shoe boxes, lugged them back.

"It's not usually this crazy," I told him.

"Don't matter to me."

"It's a better place than what you're seeing."

"I don't see anything." He took the list Murray handed him and walked off.

What's your game, Tanner?

Other Gladstone stores were having the same problems; upset store managers were calling Mrs. Gladstone to please *do something*.

"I've talked to Ken," she told each one. "He's sensitive to our growing pains, but he feels this is the best way to go. I'm not running the show anymore."

She stood by the window in her office; afternoon shadows played across the room. "The new shipment of shoes came in," I said.

"And . . . ?"

"Well, they're kind of flimsy." The term Murray used was "a joke."

"And have we heard anything back on the quality report I requested?"

"No."

40

I'd called Ken Woldman's assistant, who sounded irritated that I was checking up.

"And, Mrs. Gladstone, Helen Ruggles called from the Oakbrook store." Helen Ruggles was a top store manager. "She said she needs to come in and talk to you about—"

"This nonsense?" Mrs. Gladstone turned sharply from the window.

"Yes, ma'am."

"Tell her we'll come to Oakbrook, Jenna. I need a fresh perspective."

Early morning, I'm behind the wheel of the Cadillac, taking the open road to Oakbrook—at least metaphorically. I was actually on I-290 West, the Eisenhower Expressway, which was bumper-to-bumper traffic. Why they call this time of day *rush hour* is beyond me. It's impossible to rush anywhere.

Mrs. Gladstone was saying how there's power in numbers and if enough Gladstone managers were upset, we might be able to influence Ken Woldman, a numbers man through and through.

"We must move with speed," she said just as the traffic broke free at Harlem Avenue. I smiled, gunned the accelerator.

"Speed of purpose, dear!"

I applied the brake. "Sorry."

The Oakbrook Gladstone's Shoe Store was all windows facing a little garden of red geraniums. Everything about it seemed so sure, so right, except the window sign.

Rollings Walkers were the shoes that were giving me blisters.

Helen Ruggles, normally a happy woman, today looked stern. We sat in the back and got down to business. Helen said, "Madeline, I believe Elden wants to shut the Gladstone stores down one by one and move everything over to discount retailing."

She had to be kidding!

Mrs. Gladstone sipped her coffee. "Did he tell you that?"

Helen set her jaw. "No, but I've been hearing things. In Louisiana, Elden is exclusively selling the Shoe Warehouse labels. In Kansas City, he has just made a decision to close that store and have the local Shoe Warehouse handle the business."

Mrs. Gladstone tensed. "That's outrageous! Why haven't I been informed?"

Helen kept her voice low. "Madeline, are they taking you seriously in Dallas?"

That caught Mrs. Gladstone up short.

Helen pushed back her bangs. "I know you were named Director of Quality Control. Are they really giving you that authority?"

"Ken and I talk regularly. He's listening to my thoughts on doing business."

Helen sighed. "Elden is coming out to visit the stores and tell us about the new plan. Did you know that?"

"No," she said quietly. "I didn't."

I wasn't sure what to say on the way home.

I pulled onto I-88 and headed to Chicago. "Mrs. Gladstone," I asked finally, "what are you going to do?"

"Jenna, sometimes in life we have to fight for what we've been given. Do you understand what I mean?"

I wasn't sure why you'd have to fight for something you already had. "I don't think so."

"You see, the sad truth is that corporations can play games with people. They tell you that you have certain authority and then, without telling you, they make sure you don't."

"I had a friend like that once, Mrs. Gladstone. She kept telling me we were such good friends, but behind my back she was putting me down every chance she got."

"And what did you do about that friend?"

"I confronted her. I told her I knew what she'd been saying."

"I think I'm getting ready to do something like that, too."

"Well, don't expect people to take it real well right off, Mrs. Gladstone. Franny started screaming at me right by my locker that I was a liar. You know, it was kind of embarrassing, but then I realized it made her look like the fool, not me. That was a year ago; we still go to the same school, but she just looks away when she sees me coming."

"I will remember that, Jenna."

The longer I'm in the business world, the more I see how much they need me.

"Right now," she continued, "we have two ways to approach the matter. Retreat or advance." I could hear her sitting up straighter. I wondered how she kept going forward with all the junk piled in her way.

"I've never seen you retreat from anything, ma'am."

"I'm going to do my job whether they like it or not."

I smiled, but inside I felt cautious.

Could they fire her?

And if Mrs. Gladstone was gone, could they fire me?

I felt a sharp pain shoot through my heel.

I dropped Mrs. Gladstone at the store and limped to the only man in Chicago who could help me.

"Hi, Gus. I've got a problem."

A small, gnarled man was hunched over a shoe at a back table. He made a noise but didn't look up.

"Everyone who comes to me has a problem."

I took off my shoes to get his attention. "I'm being tortured here, Gus."

He walked slowly to me, grabbed my Rollings Walkers, felt the inside, tapped the toe, slammed it hard on the counter. He put it on the shelf near his window and peered at the heel.

"Okay, here's your situation. The stitching's a little wide and that's causing the heel to wobble. When did you buy these?"

"Two weeks ago. But I had another pair and they never gave me any trouble."

Gus felt the sole, sniffed it. He pushed his spectacles onto his wide forehead. "They changed it."

"No, Gus. Not this brand."

"Only evident to the trained eye. I could restitch it for you. Make it tighter."

"How much?"

Gus shook his head. "Everybody wants to know everything ahead of time. I'm not going to know the full damage until I get in there." He looked at the other shoe. "This one'll give you the same problem, but it hasn't blown yet." He stood back, thinking. "Twelve fifty, but that's an estimate."

"I'll bring them tomorrow."

"You gotta put these back on?"

I nodded.

He threw me a package of moleskin. "You should know better."

Even though I was in pain, I took the long way back to work so I could see Opal and remind her that her summer job from hell only had one more week to go. I saw the tiny Fotomat booth at the end of the block where Opal sat eight hours a day. In the early weeks she'd made the most of it and really turned on the personality. Now, the walls were closing in.

I poked my head in the booth. "How are you?"

"I'm thinking about the meaning of life, and the answer isn't in this *chamber.*"

"It could be worse. You could be Bo-Peep walking down the aisle."

"I could have a real job like you."

"You'd hate selling shoes. You'd argue with the customers."

"No, I wouldn't."

"Opal, you'd have to deal with the demanding public."

A woman poked her head in the booth and said, "My photos aren't ready until 5:00 P.M., but I was wondering if I could pick them up now."

Opal turned to me. Her eyes looked hunted. "What do you call this?"

Mrs. Gladstone was in her office with the door closed, but when she's upset, her voice really carries.

"Rollings Walkers have never had a five percent return. Never! We've always been at one percent or below. *What is happening at that Bangor plant?* . . . Well, find out and get back to me."

A return in the shoe business usually means the shoe was made badly. Rollings Walkers are our best-selling brand. I heard her slam the phone down. I went over and knocked on her door.

"What!"

I opened the door a crack so she could see me.

I walked in, took off my Rollings Walkers, and told her what Gus had said.

Mrs. Gladstone picked up my shoes, bent them hard, and bent them again.

"Is there something you want me to do, Mrs. Gladstone?"

"Yes," she ordered. "Get some better shoes and keep your eyes open."

Chapter 8

▶▶▶▶▶▶▶▶▶▶▶▶▶▶▶▶▶▶▶▶▶▶▶▶▶▶▶▶▶

You can find a lot that's wrong when you keep your eyes open.

There were staff problems—Murray couldn't find passionate shoe people to work other shifts. Nells, who replaced me when I was gone this summer, had the personality of a clam. Ginger, our weekend floater, was part snapping turtle. "I'm trying to motivate sea life here," Murray shouted. "Where are the visionaries? Where are the stars of tomorrow? In addition to you, kid."

"Thanks, Murray."

Company memos were coming in. My in-box was bulging.

From the desk of Elden Gladstone:

The design of Gladstone's popular women's penny loafers is being updated to appeal to today's fashion-conscious consumer. Please discount all remaining stock from now until the end of the year.

That's business speak for *Get rid of the old shoes. The brand is being eliminated.*

The funding was cut for the consulting podiatrist, too.

I peered in corners, eyes open.

But what did she want me to see?

The green envelope in my in-box read, *For everybody.* I opened it.

The card was hand-painted with brilliant colored flowers and butterflies. A squirrel family poked from behind a tree—they were all wearing high-top red sneakers.

The words A SECOND CHANCE curled across the top like skywriting. I opened it.

> Thank you for not just seeing our wrongdoing, but seeing
> the other part of us, too.
> Thank you for giving my brother and me a second chance.
> You have the best shoe store in the world.
>
> Your friend,
> Yaley

Below it was printed,

U RULE!
Webster T. Cobb, age 4 and 3/8

I'd never heard of a four-year-old who could write.

I felt a rustle of movement. There was Tanner. I showed him the card.

"The girl can paint."

"Yaley painted this?"

"She's the best, when she keeps her head straight."

He headed down the stairs before I could ask what he meant.

I thought about second chances and what Mrs. Gladstone had said about people learning from their mistakes. I thought about my dad—how I'd given him a thousand second chances probably, but they never did him any good.

I thought about the big second chance Mrs. Gladstone was giving Tanner. He could seem more grateful.

I went into Mrs. Gladstone's office and showed her the card. She studied it, smiling.

"Look at this detail, Jenna. She said her mother taught her."

"The mother on drugs?"

"Yes." Mrs. Gladstone put the card on her desk next to the picture of Elden in better days, when he was a smiling little boy.

I wondered how many second chances Mrs. Gladstone had already given him.

Her phone buzzed; I reached to answer it. Murray's voice burst through the receiver. "Kid, Madeline better get down here right away. There's a . . . *gentleman* to see her about Tanner."

The way Murray said *gentleman,* I could tell this guy didn't fit the bill.

I followed Mrs. Gladstone to the elevator; we took it to the sales floor.

A large, sweaty, pasty-colored man was standing at the register, jiggling a big key chain. The keys clicked together in an irritating clink.

"Madeline," Murray said, "this is Burt Odder. Tanner's *parole* officer."

Mrs. Gladstone didn't even blink. I tried to get Murray's attention, but he was looking down. If this were school, I would have stuck my hand in the air and asked the big question.

Ex-convicts have parole officers, right?

Burt Odder nodded slightly at Mrs. Gladstone and kept jiggling those keys. The front of his shirt was wet from perspiration.

"Ma'am, I'm here to tell you that I'm aware of you offering this individual a job, and while that's kindly, I need to make *you* aware that he's had five arrests in two years. He was just released from a youth prison for pickpocketing."

"I see." Mrs. Gladstone looked at Burt Odder's keys.

"I watch 'em come and go. I can tell the ones who are going to make it and the ones that nobody can help."

"How have you tried to help him, Mr. Odder?"

He smirked. "I tell him what's what, you know? I tell him the law."

"And how does that help him?"

"It means he knows what's what." Burt Odder leaned against the checkout counter like he owned the place.

"I would imagine he already knows what's what, Mr. Odder. I would imagine he would want to know how to get out of the fix he's in."

"Look, lady—"

"You can call me Mrs. Gladstone."

Burt Odder didn't like that, but she was just getting started. She narrowed her eyes and charged. "This is my store, Mr. Odder. I pay my taxes and I'm a law-abiding citizen. I can hire whomever I choose."

He wiped his sweaty forehead, but it didn't make much of a difference. "I just came to warn you, nice and friendly. My job is to protect the public, to assist ex-offenders adjusting to life in a free community, and to prevent future criminal acts." He said it like he had that memorized. "The rules are like this—if you decide to keep him employed, I can come in here at any time to check up on him. I got Judge Perrelli's personal orders that I'm to watch this one specially close." He showed her some official paper.

Mrs. Gladstone said, "Jenna, let Tanner know that Mr. Odder is here."

I headed in the back as Burt Odder said, "I don't need to talk to him now."

"No time like the present, Mr. Odder." She nodded to me. "Jenna . . ."

Burt Odder glared at me like I'd better not go back there.

Do I obey the law or The Law? I decided to obey the one who signed my checks.

I rushed into the back. Tanner was sweeping up, doing a really thorough job, too, getting all the dust balls from the corners. He probably learned good sweeping skills in prison. My warning bells were clanging.

"Listen," I said, "there's a guy out there you know."

Tanner looked concerned. "Who?"

"Um . . . Burt Odder."

Tanner threw the broom against the wall. The stick broke in two.

I stepped back. "I think you'd better come."

He didn't move.

"You did a good job on the floor, Tanner."

He clenched his fists, shoved them in his pockets. We walked out on the sales floor. Burt Odder smirked. "Okay, you know the routine."

Mrs. Gladstone snapped, "I don't know the *routine*, Mr. Odder. Explain it to me, please."

"He's gotta check in with me when I say and stay clean. Isn't that right, Cobbie?"

"Yeah. That's right."

"And we're happy to know he's going to be helping out here at the store." He said it like it was all a good joke.

Burt Odder jingled his keys, turned on his cheap plastic soles, and waddled out of the store. It was like watching a bad storm pass, hoping it hadn't left too much damage.

Mrs. Gladstone said, "Tanner, you can go back to what you were doing."

I carefully avoided the back room until we ran out of peds; unfortunately, that's where they were stored. Murray and I flipped a coin to see who would go in. I lost.

I poked my head in the door; Tanner was creating a recycling space, putting all the supplies in order. The peds were on the shelf across the room. How to build camaraderie and remain uninjured?

I did a quick dash across the floor, saying, "That guy Odder's a genuine jerk."

Tanner slammed twine and scissors on a shelf.

I reached up on the high shelf and got the peds. "That must be hard to have to report to somebody like that."

Tanner moved behind me. "What do you know about it?"

"Nothing. I was just—"

"What—trying to *help*? You want to rehabilitate me so you can put a badge on your arm, show you did your good deed for the day?"

I spun around. *"No. That's not—"*

"You got some kind of thing to prove with me?"

"That's not fair!"

"I don't come from where it's fair!"

He grabbed a box of shoes and threw it against the wall; he hurled another one, swearing. I dropped the peds, tore out of the back room, and almost crashed into Mrs. Gladstone; she'd been standing at the door.

"Jenna," she said, *"stay here."*

She marched into the stockroom. "*Mister* Cobb, I have no idea what your life has been like. I have no idea what it is like to try to play the hand you've been dealt. To tell you I understand would be an insult to you, but to excuse your behavior solely because of it discredits us both. *Pick up the shoes* and apologize to Jenna."

Tanner stood there, not moving. His breathing came in short gasps. Mrs. Gladstone didn't blink. Then Tanner bent down, slowly picked up the shoes, put them back in their boxes, and said, "Sorry."

She turned to me.

I swallowed hard. "It's okay, Tanner."

"Sorry about my language," he added to Mrs. Gladstone.

She glared at him. "I find that talk mostly tiresome and uncreative. But I do have a favorite four-letter word. Would you like to hear it?"

I took a step back.

"Work," she snapped, and threw a mop toward him. "There's one thing I know to be true for rich and poor—there's power in honest labor. I know how to teach it; I know how to make sure you are properly trained so that you can make a fair living. That is the opportunity I offer you here, but it won't be handed to you. You will have to work for it."

Tanner exhaled sharply and looked down.

"Jenna Boller has a work ethic that you would do well to emulate."

He nodded. "I guess I could sell shoes."

"That remains to be seen, young man." Mrs. Gladstone turned on her heel and hobbled off.

Chapter 9

>>>>>>>>>>>>>>>>>>>>>>>>>>>>>>

Over the next few days, I felt *observed*.

Tanner Cobb was studying my every move like a robber casing a bank. Mrs. Gladstone had set the stage, too.

"Jenna, I feel that there's much you can demonstrate to Tanner about good business sense."

I shook my head. Not me.

"I'm asking you to take him under your wing."

"I'm wingless." I put my arms firmly at my side to make the point.

"You soar more than you realize, dear. Now when you're doing something, explain the steps to him. Let him soak in the experience of how well you do your job."

It's hard to say no when a request comes wrapped in compliments.

I was standing on the sales floor with Tanner. When you do things naturally, it's hard to break them down with explanation. Like measuring feet.

Tanner was on his knees, trying to measure my right foot.

He moved the lever to the top of my big toe and studied it. "I can't tell if it's a ten or an eleven."

"It's a nine and a half. See that half line there?"

He peered at it. "You got big feet!"

"Tanner, think about how that might sound to a customer."

"You're not a customer."

"But if I were, saying a person has big feet might make them feel, you know, embarrassed."

He nodded. We tried it again; I stuck my foot in the measurer, Tanner fiddled with it. "You got interesting feet," he said, which wasn't much better.

"Tanner, it's best not to say anything about a customer's foot size or whether it's interesting or not."

"Why?"

"Because feet are . . . personal, but we don't want people to feel we're getting personal with them. You know?"

He studied the measurer and announced, "Okay, you're a nine and a half, but don't take it personally."

I closed my eyes and tried to impart great shoe truths:

Not every shoe is for every foot.

You can't sell everybody, but it doesn't hurt to try.

If a customer has smelly feet, *always* suffer silently.

I tried to tell him that when you have a job, you've got to get to work on time. He really had problems with that one. "I haven't got an alarm clock," he kept saying, like that excused being late. And then his phone would ring and he'd talk in that low, breathy voice. . . .

"Baby, I'm working . . ."

"Baby, I'll come by when I'm through. . . . Yeah, I will . . ."

"Baby, don't be mad. . . . Come on . . ."

"Tanner, we don't normally take so many personal calls at work. Maybe you'd better tell your friend not to call so much."

"I'm telling those girls not to call. They just keep after me."

How many *Baby*s have you got?

I stapled the white Lone Star in the corner of the big relief map of Texas, put five Western boots on plastic stands in front of the map, and lugged out the sign I'd made that proclaimed:

**WESTERN BOOTS
ON SALE**
20% OFF
THIS ONE'S FOR YOU, HARRY!

Tears stung my eyes, but I wasn't going to cry. I touched a stacked-heeled black boot. Harry Bender always wore cowboy boots.

He was the greatest shoe salesman in all of history.

Murray stood quietly at my side. "You know, kid, when Harry was ringing up a sale, he'd flick the corner of the credit card, make it twirl in the air, and catch it behind his back. The customers loved it."

"I hadn't heard that story, Murray."

"There are a million stories about him."

I centered the little photo of Harry in his Stetson hat laughing away. I decided that lighting a candle might be overkill.

Tanner sauntered into the store, twenty minutes late from lunch. He looked at the memorial. "What's that?"

"It's to honor a friend of ours that died," I told him. "When I line up all the men I've known in my life, Harry Bender was the best of them all. When I sell shoes, I think about how he did it and that helps me do my best."

Tanner touched the scar on his face. "The best man I knew was our neighbor, Ice. If you got locked out, he'd kick down a door for you or throw a brick through your window. He was that kind of guy."

"Kid," Murray said, "pulling from that memory won't help you in retail."

Tanner shrugged. "You line up most of the guys I know, you'd be smart to run the other way."

A small man was standing by the oxfords, but looking wistfully toward Harry's boot display.

"Can I help you, sir?" I asked. Tanner was at my elbow.

"Oh, I'm just looking." He stared longingly at the cowboy boots.

"I've seen a lot of people stand here trying to decide if they should try on a pair of boots," I said, smiling. Tanner smiled, too.

The man laughed. "Well, they're impractical. Cowboy boots . . . I mean, where would I wear them?"

I just stood there.

The man looked at Tanner. "Okay, tell me the truth. Would you wear these?"

Tanner grinned. "Are you kidding? I'd sleep in 'em, they're so cool."

That man's face beamed confidence. I already had the foot measure ready.

"I really came in for an oxford, but . . ."

Tanner looked at the oxfords and shook his head.

The man gulped.

I got the boots.

"Just step firmly in here, sir, and press your heel down."

That man started strutting around the store, stopping at every mirror. He stuck his thumb in his belt. "I'll take 'em," he said. His voice had grown deeper.

I rang him up at the counter, took twenty percent off in honor of Harry. Told him to stay safe out there. Tanner rolled his eyes at that one.

"Yep." He sauntered out the door. If we sold cowboy hats, we would have had a sale. Horses, even. I turned to Tanner. "It doesn't always go like this."

"You haven't had me to help before."

Just then, Yaley walked in.

"What are you doing here?" Tanner demanded.

"Checking up on you."

He opened his hands. "I'm here."

"I see you," she responded.

Tanner made an irritated noise and sauntered into the back.

"My job's never over with him," she said to me.

I had a memory flash. Me as a little kid checking up on Dad when he was watching TV. I'd count the number of empty beer cans by his chair. I learned to count that way. After a six-pack, he'd be drunk.

I looked at Yaley. "That's a lot of responsibility on you," I said.

She was defiant. "If I don't do it, he's gonna get cocky, and when he gets cocky he messes up."

"He gets cockier?"

"He's got *moves,* okay?"

I laughed. "I've got moves, too, Yaley. Don't worry. He's not my type."

Yaley shouldered her backpack like it held the weight of her world. "I want to talk to you more about Tanner sometime."

I'm not sure I wanted to learn a whole lot more, but I gave her my cell phone number before she left.

Chapter 10

▶▶▶▶▶▶▶▶▶▶▶▶▶▶▶▶▶▶▶▶▶▶▶▶▶▶▶▶▶▶

I was trying to think of the 12 Steps of Al-Anon as if they formed a staircase up to a place I really wanted to go. The problem was, I kept tripping on the first step.

Admit that we were powerless over alcohol and that our lives have become unmanageable.

I'll tell you, for a strong, tall, self-controlled person, that's a tough concept.

Don't powerless people get stomped on and lie down like doormats?

Don't strong people survive in this world?

But when I step back, I begin to see the meaning.

I'm not responsible for my dad's behavior. I have no power when it comes to that.

Do I want him to stop drinking?

Yes.

Can I do anything to make him stop?

No. I can only love him and speak the truth when we're together, if we ever are again.

It's a sad truth to hold on to, but truth isn't always happy or easy.

I was walking to the Art Institute to meet Yaley. I had a feeling I was about to learn more truth about Tanner Cobb than I wanted to.

Yaley was sitting on the big stone steps leading up to the Art Institute, drawing something on a pad. I paused a minute to look at the stone lions guarding the steps. They always seemed sorrowful to me—like they'd seen more in this world than they ever wanted.

A father lifted his son up on the lion's back. My dad used to do that with me when I was little. He'd put me on one lion and Faith on the other.

All of a sudden, I wanted to be a little kid again; wanted my dad to be here lifting me up on a lion.

I wanted to be rich and hire a detective to find my father and then pay the best doctors in the world to heal him.

I touched the stone-carved mane as I passed the lion; leaned in close to that noble face.

I walked over to Yaley. "Hi," I said, and sat down. "Cool scarf." She had a purple scarf woven through her hair. I peered at what she was drawing—it was a sketch of one of the lions. He was wearing sunglasses and had on high-top red sneakers. She had a thing for red sneakers. "That's great," I said. "I love the sneakers."

Yaley examined the drawing. "My grandma told me a story once about a little boy who put on his fastest shoes to run away from bad situations. He'd run until he found a place that was safe. I put sneakers in my pictures to help me remember."

She put her pencils in a case and looked toward the lion. "What I wanted to tell you about Tanner is he made a major dumb move, which is why he went to jail. He stole a wallet from a guy who happened to be a judge." She shook her head.

"A *judge's* wallet?"

"Talk about *dumb.* I told him, 'Why didn't you just tap a cop on the shoulder and ask him for *his* wallet? It would have been as stupid.' He said the judge wasn't wearing his robe, how was he to know? ' 'Cause all judges have the *look.* You've seen it enough,' I told him."

"Sounds like you know a lot about judges, too." I wondered if she'd ever been arrested.

"Grandma and I go to court with him so he won't feel alone. I draw the faces sometimes. I don't know what happened to Tanner in jail, but something did. He came back different."

"Different how?"

"Like he doesn't care."

Yaley turned to look at the entrance to the museum. Big banners hung down about the special exhibits. "I had some of my paintings up at school," she said, "but someday I want my art to be in a museum."

"I bet someday it will be."

She smiled slightly. "Maybe, but I could use some of Tanner's attitude to get there. It's good he's working at your store. I told him, 'You mess up this shoe job, you're worse than an idiot.' "

"What did he say?"

"He said he actually knew that."

"It sounds like you take care of him, Yaley."

"Somebody's got to. You should see the girls he hangs with." She looked up at the sky for the longest time. "Tanner's not really bad like some people say, Jenna."

"I believe that."

"*Promise me* you'll remember it."

I put the pair of red high-top sneakers on the athletic shoe display close to the front window and stood back.

Tanner walked on the floor and stopped dead when he saw them. He beamed a smile at me. The brightness of it reminded me of my grandmother's smile. It used to bounce off buildings when she walked down the street. We called her the human lighthouse.

Not anymore. Not since the Alzheimer's hit.

Tanner walked over to the sneakers and picked them up. "How much?" he asked.

I told him the price with the employee discount.

He shook his head. Couldn't afford it. He put the shoes back, but made sure they were centered just right.

Not that long ago, he probably would have stolen them.

Harry Bender always said that shoes could turn a life around.

I was merging onto Lake Shore Drive. Merging into heavy traffic is a lot like a company merger. Not everyone is thrilled you're there.

The man in the black Saab gunned his motor and tried to cut me off.

The woman in the Jeep Cherokee was offended that I'd actually joined her lane.

I drove twenty miles per hour toward the Sheridan Road exit, finally got off, and headed to Shady Oaks Nursing Home to see my grandmother.

But she wasn't in her room.

She wasn't in the dining hall or the lounge area or the game room.

I walked the halls; called out, "Grandma." Most of the old women looked up hopefully.

I grabbed a nurse to help me.

"Mrs. Lowman?" she called softly.

We went outside and couldn't find her.

I was close to panic.

Back inside, up the stairs, into the library.

"Grandma!"

She was sitting at a table. She hardly looked up.

I tried to catch my breath. *"We've been looking everywhere for you!"*

Her eyes gazed curiously at me without connection. It was the first time she hadn't recognized me at least a little. The truth of that pierced my heart.

"I'm Jenna," I told her. "Your granddaughter. *Remember?*"

"I'm Miranda," she said. "How nice to meet you."

Tears filled my eyes. She couldn't be getting this bad!

"I've been here with my books," she added.

I sat down. It took every ounce of strength I had to do that.

"You've got a lot of books," I said.

"Yes," she answered in a faraway voice. "I like stories."

So I told her Yaley's story.

And when it was over, she said, "I'm so glad you came to call."

"Me, too."

I took her hand. I used to have these big dreams about someone inventing an instant cure for Alzheimer's disease. I hope that will happen someday, but it won't be in time to help Grandma. Then I remembered what she used to tell me about dreaming when I was a little girl.

Some dreams are for keeping and others are for the wind to take away.

But how do you know which is which?

Al-Anon was helping me keep my head straight. I'd never thought of alcoholics as being lucky, but now I did, compared to Alzheimer's patients. At least there's hope for heavy drinkers—if they can stop, that is.

Today at the meeting, we were discussing mealtime in the alcoholic home.

That's always a touchy subject.

"I used to hate dinnertime when I was growing up," a guy said, "because my parents always fought about whether Dad should have more wine. They'd sit there angrily and I'd be trying to explain what happened at school. I'd make up all these excuses for not coming down to dinner." He looked at his very round stomach and laughed. "I was pretty skinny back then because of it."

"I just eat fast to get it over with," someone said.

"I eat standing up," said another guy.

"I eat walking down the street."

"I eat here." A woman tore open a Hershey's bar.

"You should have brought some for everyone, Katie."

"I ate it on the way over."

I could relate. I had my own weakness—doughnuts. Dad used to eat them when he was hung over. I'd join him, too. I can make quick work of a box of doughnut holes.

Digging around in the past always makes me hungry.

The meeting closed. The Serenity Prayer took on new meaning. I accepted the things I could not change. I simply had to have a doughnut.

I was in line at Duran's Doughnuts; it's the best blow-out treat in Chicago. Raspberry cream doughnuts, semisweet chocolate chip, applesauce raisin—one bite, and you're ruined. No other doughnut will ever do again.

The woman in front of me couldn't make up her mind. The tall guy waiting on her was patient. "You want to try an assortment?"

"I'm not sure."

"You want to zero in on our two best-selling brands?"

"I'm not sure."

Selling doughnuts could be a lot like selling shoes. Mel, the owner, waited on me. "You're looking pretty svelte there," he said to me. "You've not been in here too much."

I smiled. "I've been dieting, Mel."

"Don't go crazy with that."

I ordered two raspberry creams and a caramel pecan. I'd hit massive sugar shock in approximately an hour.

The room wasn't exactly turning, but my blood sugar had topped out. I was about to take a break when a girl with long hair and spiked heels burst through the glass doors and struck a pose. Her earrings clinked together like wind chimes.

"Tanner here?" She had the kind of voice that's all attitude.

I smiled. "I'll get him. Who should I say is—"

She laughed. "You tell him Baby's arrived."

"I'll tell him." She shook her hair like Faith does and started looking around. I poked my head in the back and sang out, "Tanner, Baby's here to see you."

Tanner peered out from the storage locker.

I grinned. "She's waiting for you."

He looked worried. "What's she look like?"

I described her.

"How tall?"

"I wasn't paying attention."

"She got a little mole above her lip?"

"I didn't get that close!"

"You tell her I was here?"

"Yes."

He shook his head, started slowly toward the sales floor like a condemned man. He walked out, half smiling, and said, "Hi, Baby, I knew you'd find me."

She gave him a fierce look. "You've been avoiding me."

"I'm working all the time."

She marched toward him, fuming. "You can't pick up the phone? I've left how many messages?"

"I don't get reception much in here."

She grabbed the phone off his belt, flipped it open. "Looks okay to me."

Tanner held out his hands and gave her a killer smile. "I do what I can with what I got."

For some reason, this calmed her. Now Tanner and Baby were talking in muffled tones. Murray stuck out his chicken neck, which meant I could take my break. Tried and true Jenna. No life beyond these walls, which was why I got so much done.

I went upstairs.

An e-mail message had come from Ken Woldman, CEO, to Mrs. Gladstone about her quality control report.

Madeline—

Great stuff. Lots to discuss on developing our common language of quality.

A package had arrived from Mergers R Hell. It had a note from Elden M. Gladstone, SI (Shoe Insect).

ALL GLADSTONE SHOE STORE PERSONNEL, REGARDLESS
OF LENGTH OF SERVICE, ARE EXPECTED TO VIEW THE
ENCLOSED SHOE WAREHOUSE CD, "HOW TO SELL A PAIR OF
SHOES." IT WILL HELP US ALL FIND THE COMMON LANGUAGE
TO MAKE THIS MERGER THE BEST IN THE BUSINESS.

"I got a bucket in case anybody needs to throw up." Murray joined me, Mrs. Gladstone, and Tanner after we closed the store. I put the CD into my computer.

Dumb music played.

A man and a woman on the screen, wearing matching Shoe Warehouse shirts. The woman said stiffly, "How do I sell a pair of shoes, Don? This is my first day." She looked pretty excited about it.

Murray gripped my chair.

"Don't worry, Suzie," said Don. "Selling shoes is as easy as one, two, three."

Tanner snorted. Mrs. Gladstone sat down. I was already sitting.

"You see, Suzie, people just want to see a friendly face when they come into a shoe store. That's the first thing you've got to remember."

Suzie nodded. "Okay, Don, I think I can remember *that*."

"And the second thing you've got to remember is that every foot is a little different." He held up a foot measurer. "That's why we have *this*!"

Tanner was laughing big time; Murray was praying, "Oh, God . . . oh, God . . ."

It went on to show Don measuring Suzie's foot and Suzie getting happier and happier as she saw that any brain-dead moron could sell shoes. You didn't have to know anything about the brands. You didn't even have to be breathing—you could be animatronic, like Don.

Tedious twerp music played as Don walked Suzie through the shoe store, finishing up with point number three. "To find the right fit, check the toe."

"What about the width?" Murray screamed. *"What about heel placement?"*

But Don didn't care about that. He shook Suzie's hand and told her she was ready to begin her exciting new career selling shoes. The CD ended.

Mrs. Gladstone went into her office and shut the door.

Murray went into the bathroom.

Tanner said, "So when am I gonna sell shoes? I can do *that*."

I glared at him until he went downstairs.

In my own defense, I would like to say that I did not see that stupid guy who was pulling out of the parking lot much too fast, and when I heard the sickening crack of his bumper connecting with my passenger door, I slammed on the brake and jumped out of the car.

"Okay," he said, examining my door, "it's just a scratch."

"I just got this car!"

"You should have been looking!"

"Give me a break!"

He was pretty tall and had a long face. He tried to use height over me, but I stood him toe to toe. He checked the front bumper of his van. "I'm not sure I had this dent before."

I looked at all the other dents on his van. "How could you tell?"

He bent down and looked at my door. "It scratched the paint. That's all."

I sputtered, "I think we should call the police." That's what you're supposed to do when you're in an accident.

"For this?" He looked at me like I was an overly emotional female, wrote out his name and number on a card, and handed it to me.

CHARLIE DURAN
Home: 555-1744
Work: 555-1600

The card was from Duran's Doughnuts. Believe me, doughnuts were the only thing this guy had going for him. I wrote my name on a Gladstone's card.

"Good store," he said. "Look, if you want to call the police, can we call them tomorrow? I've got to get to school."

It's seven o'clock at night. What kind of school do you go to?

He climbed into his van without waiting for my answer and drove off.

What a jerk.

I was fuming when I got home and called Opal. She was all a-flutter about this French guy who stopped by the Fotomat booth. "I feel *total* chemistry with him, Jenna. Complete and utter connection."

"What's his name?"

"I don't know."

"What did you talk about?"

"How much it costs to get a roll of fast-speed color film developed. He came back three times. But, believe me, the most important thing was there."

Chemistry is high on Opal's list of relationship necessities. It's number two, actually, wedged between #1—Undying Devotion, and #3—Blind Loyalty. Sometimes I wonder if Opal should just get a dog.

I told her about Charlie Duran, Doughnut Dope. Opal jumps to conclusions in her own life much quicker than in mine.

"Jenna," she said finally, "if it's only a scratch, you should probably let it go."

"But I feel like he scratched a part of me."

"I know, but he didn't. And your insurance premium would go up if you make a claim and he makes one against you. A scratch isn't permanent, Jenna; a higher premium is forever."

Chapter 11

▶▶▶▶▶▶▶▶▶▶▶▶▶▶▶▶▶▶▶▶▶▶▶▶▶▶▶▶▶▶▶▶▶▶

Over the next three days, Mrs. Gladstone had an idea that turned into a full-fledged brainstorm.

"Best foot forward," she said to me. "What does that mean to you?"

I smiled. "My grandma used to say that to me every year on the first day of school. She'd tell me to put my best foot forward and try to do my best."

"I would have liked your grandmother."

"You would have, Mrs. Gladstone. She was a pistol." I grinned. "Like you."

Mrs. Gladstone's face was flushed with the energy of a new idea.

"Now this best foot forward, Jenna. I'm thinking that could be the slogan for the merger of our two companies. I've been trying to figure out how we pull from the best of what we both offer." She shuddered. "Not the worst."

Our CEO, Ken Woldman, loved the idea and he called the

advertising agency, who thought it made a good slogan. Best foot forward was taking hold. My grandmother was getting me ready for this job without either of us knowing it.

But not everyone was committed to doing their best. Tanner Cobb seemed to think that a one-hour lunch break meant that he could be gone for one and a half hours and no one would notice.

I confronted him. "Tanner, you can't be late from lunch every day."

"I haven't got a watch," he said.

"Then you've got to look for clocks. Chicago has a lot of clocks."

"I'm not so good at getting places on time."

"There are ways to get better."

Just then a tall, pretty girl walked into the store. Her eyes turned to slits when she saw Tanner.

"Save me, save me," he whispered to me.

What was he talking about? She marched toward him.

He rubbed the scar on his face. "Hi, Denise."

"I thought you left town."

More rubbing. "I did for a while."

"Why didn't you call me?"

"I been working, Baby."

She didn't buy that. Smart girl. "How long you been working?"

Tanner looked pleadingly at me.

"I'm new here, Baby, but, you know, work's intense. It doesn't let up."

He had that right. I said, "We're going to have to do that work in the back, Tanner."

"I'll call you," he told her.

She glared at him.

Give it up, Denise.

She stood there as the truth hit and shook her head sadly. "Just forget it." She headed for the door.

Tanner shrugged; forgetting it wasn't hard for him. He did a half spin around like a dancer and headed for the back room.

Why did my life suddenly feel so crushingly dull?

"I'm back, everybody! And I'm getting shoes!"

Webster T. Cobb burst through the door, grinning wide, followed by his grandmother.

"Good to see you, Webster."

"I want tie-ups!"

"We've got those."

He headed toward the children's section; checked the tree to make sure his name was still there; grabbed a squirrel. Mattie shook my hand. "He wouldn't come anyplace else. He said this was his shoe store."

Webster did a half spin like Tanner. "I've got awesome feet."

I laughed. "You sure do. Come on, let me measure you."

"I'm three feet tall exact."

"Not your height, your feet."

Mattie bent closer to me. "We're going to have to go with the economy brand."

"Employees get a discount." I got Webster to stand still momentarily while I got his size, then found cool tie-ons from the sales rack suitable for awesome feet. I stuck the shoes on Webster. He laced them up himself slowly and ran around the store.

"You've got to give them a good test," I said. "Run, march, bounce, and jump. It's the only sure way to tell."

Mattie smiled. "I want to thank you for what you're doing for my grandson."

"Webster is a special kid."

"Not him," she said. *"Tanner."*

Tanner?

"He looks up to you."

Most guys do. I'm five-eleven.

"He says you know what's what."

"He's a good worker."

"He needed this job like a lifeline. I've been praying for that boy to get a break, and look where he is. You're God's agent. Do you know that?"

Is she kidding?

"Oh, yes you are. I got on my knees for that boy and asked the Lord to provide. And he sent you."

Webster did a somersault and landed right at our feet. "I want these, Grandma! They're the best!"

"How much are they?"

As God's agent, I gave her a double discount and threw in

two pairs of iridescent laces. Tanner came on the floor as I was ringing them up. Webster marched up to him. "I read two whole books today."

"That's good, little man. You learn any new words?"

Webster thought hard. "I don't think so."

"I got a new word for you." Tanner went behind the counter, got a piece of paper and a pen, and wrote out SOLE. "Sole," he said.

Webster wasn't impressed. "I know that one! We say it in church."

"It sounds like the church word; that's spelled S-O-U-L. This one means the bottom of your shoe. That's the sole. S-O-L-E."

Webster took off his new shoes and examined the bottoms. "Sole," he said.

Tanner did a full turn and stuck his hands out like a dancer. "And 'cause I work in a shoe store, I'm a sole man!"

Webster did a half turn and posed. "I'm a sole man, too!"

Mattie paid for the shoes. "We've got to go, honey."

Webster was too busy to pay attention. She marched over to him, took his hand.

"No," he insisted. "I want to stay."

Mattie bent down and said something to him I couldn't hear. Webster shook his head.

"We've got to go, honey. That's just how it is."

"We live in a basement apartment. The mildew keeps the rent cheap. Webster's allergic to it. He doesn't like going back." Tanner and I stood on the sales floor next to Harry's memorial.

"Allergies can be tough," I said. "I had them pretty bad when I was little, but I grew out of them." I considered my height and laughed. "I grew out of just about everything."

"We had to move fast from our other place 'cause my father's *business associates* kept coming by, hassling us."

What kind of business were *they* in?

"My old man's in the joint." He squared his shoulders when he said it.

"I heard. I'm sorry. Do you mind me asking what he's in for?"

"Assault and battery, robbery, resisting arrest, assaulting an officer, possession of narcotics, unlawful possession of a firearm . . ."

I think he could have kept going. "Will he be getting out anytime . . . soon?"

"You mean, is he gonna come visit me at the store?"

I straightened the cowboy boots on the display. "I was just . . . curious . . ."

"When he gets out, I'll probably be thirty. If he behaves himself, which he never does." Tanner stood there staring at the Lone Star, the unifying symbol of Gladstone Shoes and all of Texas.

"My dad was in jail, but only for a couple of days." I gulped, not sure why I said this.

"What for?"

"Drunk driving."

Tanner snorted.

"It seemed like a pretty big thing to me."

He laughed. "I'm here to remind you there's always somebody worse off."

"You win," I said. "So, what's it like for you with your dad? Do you see him?"

He picked up the photo of Harry Bender. "Nah, I don't see him."

He stood there studying Harry's face. "You want to know what my old man's like? The bank's got a video of him taking money and beating up a guard, and he claims he's innocent. He's been in and out of drug clinics for years and he says he's not hooked."

"My dad has trouble with truth, too."

"I tell Webster, when you aim at zero, you always hit the mark." He put the picture back. "I'm learning about aiming better." He laughed. "Mrs. G's a good shot."

"You mean metaphorically?"

"Yeah. Whatever."

That's when Charlie Duran pushed through the door.

What was *he* doing here?

He looked right at me. "Is it crimson red or burgundy?"

"*What* are you talking about?"

He shouldered his book bag. "What color is your car? I got a paint card from the dealer. I'm not sure which red you've got." He held out the card with five squares of different reds. "I'm trying to get the right paint to match your car so I can fix the scratch."

It took a minute for that to sink in.

"I wasn't looking, either," he said.

I stood there.

Tanner looked at me. "Uh . . . I don't have my car here today."

"Bring it tomorrow and I'll see if I can match the paint."

"I guess."

"Okay, I'll see you." Charlie Duran looked around. "Nice store," he said, and headed out. He had broad shoulders—broader than mine, even.

"Who was that?" Tanner asked.

I cleared my throat. "A doughnut guy."

Tanner nodded like that made perfect sense.

I went back to what I was doing, but I couldn't remember what that was.

There's not that much difference between crimson red and burgundy. Charlie Duran asked five complete strangers in the parking lot which color they thought was the best match. Crimson won, three to two.

"I thought that was it." He took a little bottle of crimson paint and painted over the scratch on my door. "Good as new," he said.

"Thanks." I wasn't used to looking up at guys when I talked to them.

I asked him about school—he was just starting at Palmer Junior College, taking night classes in business so he could work days.

We talked about the rigors of retail—he'd been working in

stores since he was a little kid. When he lived in Indiana, his other grandfather owned a White Hen.

"Okay, so . . . we'll talk again." He smiled. Doughnut people are refreshingly straightforward.

"Sure," I said casually, tossing my hair and getting some of it in my mouth.

He handed me four Duran's Doughnuts coupons and left.

I called Opal.

"Okay, Jenna, you're doing pretty well, but your voice sounds like you're having trouble breathing."

"I am a little. . . ." I mentioned the coupons.

"Don't use those coupons," she said. "Let him come to you."

"You're kidding? These are two for the price of one, Opal!"

"You've got to be casual and distant, Jenna. It's the only way these days."

"What about you and Jacques?"

"*He* comes to the Fotomat booth to talk, Jenna. And he's getting ready to ask me out."

"How can you tell?"

"He asked me when I got off work *in French.*"

I put the doughnut coupons in my pocket and sighed.

I can't tell you how much I wanted a raspberry cream.

Chapter 12

>>>>>>>>>>>>>>>>>>>>>>>>>>>>>>>

The puffy foot costume arrived at Gladstone Shoes. I took it out of the box; it was tan colored with prominent toes. It had a head hole and came with tan tights. On the front of it was written, PUT YOUR BEST FOOT FORWARD.

It's amazing how an advertising agency can destroy a good idea.

"I'm not wearing it." I said this firmly, embracing Al-Anon boundary-setting principles.

Murray pushed back the two head hairs he had left. "I'm sure not wearing it."

Tanner was rushing through the front door, late again. He stared at the costume, felt the puffy material. "You'd get shot wearing this in my neighborhood."

The puffy foot costume was part of a big Labor Day Blowout Sales Extravaganza we were going to have at the Shoe Warehouse Corporation's 498 stores across America: 498 puffy feet were going to march into malls and streets to wave, pass out coupons, and overwhelm America. Getting ready for a big sale wasn't easy. We'd lugged hundreds of shoes from the stockroom and put them on shelves. We'd hung the Best Foot Forward banner across the ceiling.

"We could say it didn't come," Murray offered.

I put the costume down. "I signed for the package with UPS."

"We could maybe pay my nephew Lyle to wear it," Murray offered, "but if it's not hypoallergenic, in ten minutes he'd be spitting up phlegm."

"There's a bonus for whoever wears it," Mrs. Gladstone added, coming up from behind.

Tanner stepped forward. "What would my bonus be?"

Mrs. Gladstone cleared her throat. "A watch—which, young man, you could sorely use—and overtime pay."

"I got to wear the tights?"

"I'm afraid so."

"Can I wear my shades?" Tanner put on his mirrored sunglasses, raised his hands like a dancer, and froze.

Mrs. Gladstone's smile broke wide open. "I think they would greatly add to the depth of your characterization."

Tanner put his best foot forward and stood on Wabash Street outside Gladstone Shoes and almost caused a riot. He was bowing to people, blowing kisses to women, patting little kids on the head, and handing out the coupons.

"What are you, man?" a teenage guy asked Tanner.

"I'm a foot fetish," Tanner explained.

"No!" I shouted. "He's just kidding." I glared at Tanner's face poking from the head hole; saw myself mirrored back. I hate mirrored sunglasses.

"I'm the Best Foot Forward," Tanner said obediently and handed the guy a coupon. "And this is your lucky day."

"Are you a right foot or a left foot?" a little girl asked him.

Tanner looked at the toes protruding out from his knees. "I'm a right foot."

She squeezed his puffy big toe. "Do you feel stupid?"

"Yeah, I sure do!"

"Do you know Ronald McDonald?" another kid asked.

We hadn't covered these questions in training. "Are you kidding?" Tanner replied. "Ron lives next door to me. We hang out."

"You know Mickey Mouse?"

A crowd was gathering.

"I know him. I'm the Foot, you understand? They all come to me." Tanner gave a coupon to every person and this mass of humanity headed into the store. I followed them. A sea of customers clutching coupons rifled through the sales shelves, trying on shoes, leaving boxes piled on the floor. The line at the register was curling through the store and Mrs. Gladstone was ringing people up like a machine.

I've been through enough sales at this store—the Spring Fling, the Holiday Magic, the End of the Year Closeout—but I'd never seen numbers like this.

It was hard to keep an eye on everything, hard to help when people didn't know what they wanted themselves. Customers were leaning against the wall to try shoes on. There was no place left to sit. Tanner moved among his fans like a rock star and walked a few inside.

Then a rustle in the back. Tanner shouted, "*Stop it,* man!"

A panicked guy started pushing toward the front door, holding a box.

Tanner lunged after him, puffy toes swinging. "Hold it!"

I was by the door. The guy ran close to me, I stuck out my right foot, and he went crashing down.

"*I was going to pay for it!*"

"Yeah? *When?*"

The guy kicked him; Tanner pinned him down and shoved his knee with the protruding toes into the guy's chest as Murray called the police. But Gladstone customers are tough and dedicated. They kept shopping, clutching their coupons, keeping a wide berth around Tanner and the shoplifter. The police came and walked the guy off.

"Only in America," Murray said afterward, shaking his head.

I looked at Tanner, saw that scar running down his face; his glasses were off, his dark eyes burning. If there was any doubt about whether he was one of us, that doubt was gone now. He was a sole man through and through.

The day after Labor Day, to celebrate the great Best Foot Forward campaign that was hugely successful across the country, and to show the unity and spirit alive in the newly merged Shoe Warehouse Corporation, Ken Woldman laid off 304 people nationwide. "We will continue to combine operations and to pass that cost savings onto our customers," he said as if he'd just done something to help mankind. Mrs. Gladstone was furious at the news.

"*What* is that man thinking?" she shouted, shut herself in her office, and called him.

Murray was having nightmares that he was going to be the 305th to go. I tried to tell him Mrs. Gladstone would protect him, but Murray said the company was changing too fast.

"I'm a dead man, kid."

I couldn't imagine the store without Murray.

I couldn't imagine the store without me, but Gladstone's was going to have to get used to me being gone, at least part-time. Murray was interviewing for part-time help. He faced a young woman and threw out his make-or-break question:

"Okay, say six customers come into the store at once; they all want to be waited on pronto; they start getting surly. What do you do?"

She looked at him. "I'd tell them to wait their turn and if they didn't like it, tough."

That's the wrong answer.

Murray had asked me that question at my interview, too. I'd said, "I'd tell them help was on the way, and come and find you." His face went soft when I said it.

"We'll call you," Murray said to the young woman.

Just then the UPS man lugged in an enormous box and laid it down. "What's in this thing?"

Murray and I opened the box. Inside was a large gong-shaped bell with the Shoe Warehouse emblem.

Murray looked at it with hunted eyes. "Who knows for whom the bell tolls, kid. It tolls for me." He bonged the bell in grief.

Tanner ran onto the sales floor. *What was that?*

"The future," Murray said miserably.

Chapter 13

>>>>>>>>>>>>>>>>>>>>>>>>>>>>>

School was starting tomorrow. One day left of freedom.

Opal and I were standing at Belmont Harbor, watching the sailboats. A long sailboat moved slowly out to the lake; three people manned it. There are some things you can't do yourself—you need other people to help you.

This was one of those times for me. "I've been reading in my Al-Anon book," I began, "and I'm learning how sometimes it's hard for kids with alcoholic parents to have"—I winced—"fun." I stood there desperately trying to appear fun-loving.

Opal examined me. "You could definitely use more fun in your life, Jenna."

A kid glided by effortlessly on a skateboard. "So, how do I do that?"

"You want to skateboard?"

"No, I mean, general fun. How do I enter into that?"

Opal started laughing. "You start by smiling."

I laughed, kind of.

"And you stop taking yourself so seriously."

That stopped me laughing. All my life people have told me I'm too serious. I was a serious baby, a serious toddler, a serious preschooler.

"What do you think is fun?" she asked.

I looked around. This was the difficult part. "Don't laugh," I said. "Promise."

Hand over her heart.

"I think selling shoes is a lot of fun."

She cracked up.

"Okay, Opal. Brace yourself. I think that washing my car is fun. *And* I think driving is fun and it's more fun when the car is clean."

She was guffawing now.

"I thought you liked my car!"

"Jenna, this is serious. Do you ever do things on the spur of the moment?"

"Sure." My mind stretched trying to think of them. I mentioned renting a movie on the absolute spur of the moment and cooking.

She took my arm and yanked me deeper into the park.

"Okay, Jenna, stand on that rock and scream."

"Why?"

"Because it frees your inhibitions."

"I like my inhibitions."

"Just try it."

I stood on the rock and gave a short, soft shout.

"How did that feel?"

"Boring."

Opal stood on the rock, threw back her head, and bellowed. Birds flew out of the trees, squirrels ran for cover. Her face looked peaceful when she was through.

I threw back my head and shouted louder. I let my hands go up and down and the shout grew within me. I shrieked.

But honestly, it didn't do much for me.

I liked to work. I liked to be purposeful.

Opal shook her head. "Jenna, you're probably going to be one of the top businesspeople in America."

I grinned. Now *that* would be fun.

The first day of school came down hard like a big boot from above.

The best part of the day was how many people came up and told me I looked good. I tossed my head and felt my new wispy bangs play across my face. I was wearing green, the color of new life.

It was amazing how much I'd changed over the summer and how my classmates had not. Matt Wicks, who I'd had a crush on all sophomore year, seemed childish and boring. I felt like I was living out one of those fantasy movies where the sharp adult gets zapped back into childhood and has to go back to school and relive what was not worth reliving.

Journalism with Mr. Haloran was worth the experience, though, because Mr. Haloran had the deepest, bluest eyes in all of education.

I held the sheet he passed out with the four questions we always had to ask before turning in a paper to him:

Are the facts confirmed?

Is the writing clear?

Is the piece informative?

Will Mr. Haloran unconditionally love this?

I had my own questions for the school year:

Can I . . .

Maintain a B average?

Have a balanced life?

Survive?

I raced into Gladstone's and paused for a moment of silence at Harry Bender's memorial.

If life were close to fair, Harry would have been my father. He would have driven my mother up the wall, and it's safe to say that Faith wouldn't have turned out nearly as pretty, but that's a small price to pay for all the insight he would have shared.

Then the sound of jingling keys.

Burt Odder thumped into the store and plopped his damp body into a chair.

He was rubbing his calf, not surprising, looking at those old shoes he was wearing. He got up and I could see a gentle limp when he walked over to the men's loafers.

Everything within me wanted to ignore him, but I thought, okay.

This one's for you, Harry.

Harry always said you had to treat each customer like a friend.

I marched over to him, smiling. "I bet you're on your feet a lot during the day," I said.

"You got that right." He didn't look at me when he said it.

I picked up an excellent shoe that was dirt cheap on special because we only had wide sizes left. He had a wide foot. I told him about the depth of the cushioning and the ease of the walk and how the insoles massage the foot.

"You got it in twelve wide?"

"Let's just measure you to be sure."

He sat down and took off his shoe, and instantly I regretted this whole thing, because this man had foot odor that could knock you senseless. Murray always told me to move to the side of a person to avoid the direct fumes. My eyes were tearing, but I got him up on the measurer. "I think you're a twelve and a half, actually." I looked at his shoes that were almost bursting out at the little toe from the pressure. "Let me see what I've got."

I went in the back, grabbed the twelve and a half wides, did some deep breathing to fill my lungs with clean air, and hurried back on the floor. He was waiting there, kind of docile. It's amazing how people respond to having someone address their foot issues. I put the shoes on him.

He stood up and almost smiled. "Are these too loose? I can wiggle my toes."

"You're supposed to be able to do that."

"Really." He walked around a little bit. "How much?"

I told him the super sale price.

"Yeah. Yeah, I'll take them."

Just then, Tanner walked out. Tanner stopped short when he saw him. I wasn't sure what to do, so I just kept going with the transaction. Did he want to pay cash or credit?

I took his Visa card, rang it up.

Burt Odder signed the receipt. I said, "You're going to love those shoes. They were made for you."

He looked right past me to Tanner. "Give me a little tour."

"There's nothing to see."

"I'll be the judge of that."

Murray came out on the floor. "I'll take you back there."

"I want to see where he works."

Murray led the way. Tanner and I followed into the storage room.

"Empty your pockets, Cobbie boy."

Tanner didn't move.

"Empty them."

Tanner took out keys, some coins, a battered wallet. Burt Odder moved forward, patted the side of Tanner's pants. "What you got in there?"

"Nuthin'."

"Let's see that nuthin'."

Tanner shook his head, put his hand in the side pocket, and pulled out a Snickers bar.

Odder picked up Tanner's torn book bag. "This yours?"

Tanner looked like he was going to punch his fist through a wall.

"I asked you a question."

"It's mine."

"Everything out."

How humiliating.

Tanner took out paper, pens, a bag of chips.

Burt Odder grabbed the bag, turned it upside down. Out fell an expensive pair of men's snakeskin boots.

My breath caught in my throat.

"Well, now." Burt Odder picked up a boot. "Very nice. This yours, Cobbie?"

Tanner looked down.

I turned around and saw Mrs. Gladstone leaning on her cane, watching in steely silence.

"You got a receipt for these?" Odder picked up the other boot.

Tanner said nothing.

"I told you, ma'am, this kid was no good."

"Yes, you told me."

"Well, we're just going to take him off your hands and put him right back where he belongs."

"But, you see," Mrs. Gladstone said matter-of-factly, "I gave those to Tanner."

What did she say?

"I gave the boots to him," she repeated.

Tanner looked as shocked as anyone.

"There was no crime here," she added.

Burt Odder sputtered, "Lady, do you know what you're doing?"

She stood defiantly. "Is there anything else you'd like to see, Mr. Odder?"

Odder's face flamed fire red. He gave a disgusted grunt and stormed out.

Mrs. Gladstone said, "Jenna, I'd like to speak to Tanner alone, please."

I backed out of the room.

"It was wrong what I did."

Tanner said it from behind me. I didn't turn around.

"I don't know why I did it."

"I don't either, Tanner."

"What should I do next?"

"I have no idea."

"Mrs. G said you'd tell me what to do next!"

I turned around, saw his face caved in with what? Guilt? Shock that he got away with it *again?*

"I don't know what you and Mrs. Gladstone talked about, Tanner. Maybe you should just go home."

He forced a smile. "Your eyes look great when you get—"

"Don't!"

I turned away as he ran out the door.

Chapter 14

▷▷▷▷▷▷▷▷▷▷▷▷▷▷▷▷▷▷▷▷▷▷▷▷▷▷▷▷▷▷

"I owe you an explanation, Jenna." Mrs. Gladstone stood before me, lips pursed tight.

"No, you don't."

"I gave Tanner a second chance because I didn't think justice would be served through that reprehensible Odder person."

Justice? "He stole from us after everything you did for him. What makes you think he won't do it again? He tricked all of us!"

"Did he trick us, Jenna, or did he fall into his old patterns? He was like a sponge in this place, soaking everything up. This job has been crucial to him."

"I'm sorry, Mrs. Gladstone. That doesn't excuse it."

I was sick of excuses. My dad had all the excuses in the world.

"You're right," she agreed, "but Tanner did not come here with your discipline."

I sighed. "You've sure got a nicer view of humanity than me."

"I've just lived longer. If Tanner does come back, I'm hoping we can all meet him halfway."

"I don't know if I can."

"I'm asking a lot of you. I know that." Her face got faraway. "My father always said that to me. I chafed at being a preacher's kid. I watched him practice grace every day with people I thought were unworthy of his efforts."

I wasn't in the mood to debate. "You're the boss, Mrs. Gladstone."

"Yes, but my authority does not extend to the heart."

I bet she could order hearts around if she set her mind to it.

"Jenna, I don't know if we'll ever see Tanner Cobb again, but I'm betting that if he comes back, he won't steal."

"What if you're *wrong*, Mrs. Gladstone? *What do we do then?*"

She just stood there, all spine—a short monument to women of steel.

The problem with the heart is how it can have so many opposite feelings coursing through it at the same time. It's really an inconsistent thing—appreciating something one minute, hating it the next. Tanner had left the store two days ago and we'd not seen or heard from him since. I was so glad when he left. Now I was thinking about what Yaley had said.

Tanner's not bad like some people say, Jenna.

Promise me you'll remember it.

When Yaley called and asked what happened, I told her.

Mattie came in the store, saying she was as sorry as she'd ever been for what Tanner did.

You can't fix it for him, I wanted to shout.

I was trying to handle homework, trying to be strong. I wrote out a schedule for myself. If every single moment went perfectly, if I cut back on sleep and never missed a green light, I'd be fine.

I was answering the phone, taking messages from anxious store managers. Two more called saying that Elden was due in town tomorrow to talk about changes in their stores, and what were they supposed to do?

Mutiny?

Saturday, 8:47 A.M. I pulled into the parking lot behind the Oak Park Gladstone's store. Mrs. Gladstone had brought her cane for the occasion—not just for emphasis; her hip was getting worse. Elden's meeting was due to start in thirteen minutes. He didn't know we were coming, but, hey, we're all one big happy family. Right?

Dick McAllister, the store manager, met us at the back door, looking grim. "He's got a PowerPoint presentation," he said. "But worse than that . . ." Dick held up a green shirt with the Shoe Warehouse emblem. "I'm not wearing this, Madeline."

I'm not, either.

Elden was shouting out instructions for how the screen was to be displayed for his presentation. He had his back to us, but it's said that snakes can sense prey, even in the tall weeds. He turned around and froze when he saw us.

"Well, Elden," Mrs. Gladstone said, walking toward him. "Haven't you been a busy bee?" Her cane clicked on the floor. Elden tried to find his voice.

"Mother." He tried to smile.

"I'm here for your presentation," she said, and sat down.

I sat down next to her. "Hello, sir."

"Oh," he said, *"you."*

The one and only. And even smarter since I last saw you.

More shoe people came in the door. Elden had invited most of the Gladstone's managers throughout the western suburbs. He busied himself with the people who came in. Dick McAllister put up folding chairs nervously; everyone got coffee. Helen Ruggles sat next to Mrs. Gladstone. "You're looking tougher than ever, Madeline."

That got a smile.

"Well," Dick McAllister said, "I know we're all anxious to hear from you, Elden."

Elden slithered forward and said, "We are embarking on a bold new journey that I believe will put Gladstone's in the forefront of shoe companies worldwide."

He clicked to his first slide, which read, Change Is Good.

Elden then went on to explain how the Shoe Warehouse design for effective retailing would be our design as well. He showed the new plans for our stores—each store would look exactly alike. "No more worrying about how to design the displays," he chirped. "That will be done for you." The managers slumped glumly in their seats.

So much for creativity.

"We are in the age of instant information," Elden continued. "And Ken Woldman understands that people get bored with the same old thing. That's why we'll have daily sales, even hourly specials—an exciting, ever-changing sales environment."

He clicked to the next slide: Change Is Exciting.

"We will be installing closed-circuit TVs in twenty of our flagship stores and experimenting with how to get as much information to our customers as we can."

Elden smirked. "Ken has asked that *I* be the spokesman. We're going to broadcast our bargains to our customers day and night!" His voice got a little lower, like a DJ. "Along with some special shoe and fashion tips!"

He showed a store design with the huge TV monitor on the wall.

Despair settled over the group.

I felt like I was being sucked into the center of one of those extreme-makeover shows.

Click. Together We Will Change the World.

If we don't all die from humiliation first.

That's when Mrs. Gladstone stood up. "Elden, when do you expect Gladstone's will be entirely eliminated?"

Shock hung in the room.

He sputtered. "Mother, no one is saying that."

"When will the G be taken off the door? When will the signs be taken down? When will our brands become obsolete?

You're already making them into cheap knockoffs. Gladstone's *used* to stand for quality." She rammed her cane on the floor. *"Surely you've discussed this."*

"Mother, I hardly think—"

"I expect you've been thinking about this for quite some time, Elden." She marched forward, glaring at him.

"Well..." He put his clicker down. "I would estimate that the full changeover to the Shoe Warehouse philosophy should happen within, perhaps, the next year or so."

"And what will happen to our best-selling brands? The Rollings Walkers, for example?"

He laughed nervously. *"If* they continue to sell well, we'll keep making them, of course."

"I see." She walked to the wall and threw up the light switch. "Ladies and gentlemen, as the Director of Quality Control, I want to say publicly that I disagree with this approach. First, as a member of the board of directors, I object to my not being informed of this sudden turn in our company's direction. That is against the bylaws of our company and, therefore, I will challenge it. Ken Woldman has assured me there is room in this organization for both high-quality shoes and budget brands. I mean to hold him to his word. And as the mother of our general manager, I have one thing to say to him." I closed my eyes and heard her shout, "This will happen *over my dead body!"*

"My God, Mother!"

She pointed at the Together We Will Change the World screen. "I assure you, God Almighty had nothing to do with *that!"*

Applause began quietly at first, then more loudly.

Elden sputtered that anyone who did not go along with this new direction was welcome to turn in their resignation.

The shoe managers looked nervous and stopped clapping.

"We'll see about that!" Mrs. Gladstone nodded to me and marched out the door.

I marched after her.

The mutiny had begun.

At least I think it had.

Chapter 15

▶▶▶▶▶▶▶▶▶▶▶▶▶▶▶▶▶▶▶▶▶▶▶▶▶▶▶▶▶▶▶▶▶▶▶▶

Mrs. Gladstone and I were seated in rickety chairs in Gus's Shoe Repair. Gus held up a year-old pair of Rollings Walkers and the pair I'd brought in last week. The whole shop smelled like shoe polish.

"So," he said, "anyone who tells you they haven't changed this shoe is a liar."

Mrs. Gladstone said, "I need facts, Gus."

"I got those." He turned my pair over, flexed them. "The shoes Jenna brought in have got thermal plastic rubber bottoms. TPRs are used only in inexpensive casuals these days. See the crack there?"

We looked.

"I didn't have to work hard to get that to crack." He held up the real Rollings Walkers that Mrs. Gladstone had brought in for comparison. "These here, they're older, but they got one hundred percent rubber soles. Rubber's our friend when it comes to durability."

He yanked out the inside of my new shoe. "This isn't

leather. It's man-made. It's not going to breathe like your leather, which is what you've got on the older pair. On the outside, they don't look different. On the inside . . ." He shook his head. "It's like sirloin and Spam." He handed me back my shoes.

Mrs. Gladstone threw back her head and took a big breath.

"Madeline, it's changing everywhere. It's not just Gladstone's. I'm seeing a lot of garbage."

"I can't accept garbage, Gus."

"That's why you're the one to fight it." He patted her hand; got some shoe polish on it, but that's a mark of distinction in our world.

Back at work, Mrs. Gladstone told me to write up everything Gus had said and put it in a file. I wrote up everything I could remember Elden saying, too.

It was the end of the day. She sat in her chair looking out the window. An elevated train rumbled by. She didn't move when I came in.

"Do you want me to drive you home, ma'am?"

"Not just yet."

I'd gone the miles with this woman—seen her shot down and seen her get back up. I walked to her window and opened it. A big Chicago wind knocked her geranium plant off the sill. It crashed on the floor, but the planter didn't break.

I picked it up. "Now, that's quality."

"It is indeed," she said sadly.

"There are things that get knocked down by the wind, Mrs. Gladstone, and they don't break. They're too strong. Like you."

She tried smiling bravely, but her heart wasn't in it.

"Mrs. Gladstone, you're still Director of Quality Control. You're still on the board of directors. You've still got a voice in this company, don't you?"

"I'm not so sure."

"Well, I am. You've got a job to do. You've got to show the things that are wrong so that this company can be made better. Isn't there room for the quality brands in this new company? Isn't that why Ken Woldman wanted you in this position? Lots of people will pay the money for high-end shoes!" Dirt was getting on my clothes from the geranium, but I didn't care. "Mrs. Gladstone, other than all this mess with your son, what was the hardest thing you've had to face with the company?"

Her old head lifted; her chin got stiff.

"It was when Floyd died suddenly and I had to take the reins."

"That must have been a killer, ma'am. . . . I didn't mean it like that."

She sat there lost in thought. "I didn't know what I was doing."

"But you figured it out."

"I was the back office person, he was the one always up front."

"But you found a way."

"People didn't think I was up to it."

"But you were."

"And the memories of him in every corner . . . Lord, I didn't think I could keep going. I didn't think I could sit in his chair."

"But you did."

Her eyes narrowed, but she was smiling. "You're a very persistent young woman."

She had that right. "No disrespect, ma'am, but a wuss would get trampled in this place."

We closed the store at 7:00 P.M.

Murray stood before the bell, holding the mallet. "When you hear this sound, remember the world's gone mad."

Booonnnggg.

The *booonnnggg* was still reverberating as we walked out the door.

The pressure of schoolwork and my work schedule was building.

Would I drive Faith to school in the mornings?

Only if we're out the door by 7:00 A.M.—no excuses.

She said fine, then the excuses came.

"I can't find anything to wear."

"I couldn't get to sleep last night."

"You were in the bathroom so long this morning."

"Faith, I'm getting up at 5:30 to give you space to get ready!"

"You are so bossy, Jenna!"

Faith sat silently in the car as I hit four detours this morning. I was coming up on the Michigan Avenue bridge that arched over the Chicago River. It was close to my favorite part of the city. I thought about bridges and how they're built to connect two places and how we needed to be bridge builders in this world because there are so many places where people can't connect.

I sat in my car, boxed in by rush hour. Sat there, God's agent, without an angel or a burning spear in sight. I didn't even have good company.

I stared at the river and opened my hands. "Part," I said jokingly. "Something part and give me a break."

Faith looked at me like I was nuts.

Just then the screaming policeman who was directing traffic and making everything worse walked away in disgust. Miraculously the traffic cleared.

I glanced upward, made a left turn across the bridge, and we headed to school.

Mrs. Gladstone faced the video conferencing monitor from her office in Chicago and said to the management team assembled in Dallas, "I have a question, gentlemen."

"Go ahead, Madeline," Ken Woldman replied.

"Who authorized changing the design of the Rollings Walkers?"

The men around the table looked surprised. Elden's snake tail rattled.

Ken Woldman turned to Elden, who said he wasn't aware of any change.

"We're getting double-digit returns on that brand." She didn't mention what Gus had said.

"That's not good." Ken Woldman looked at Elden, who wrote something on a pad.

"We'll look into it, Mother."

"When can I expect the report?"

"A few weeks." Elden tapped his pen impatiently. "These things take time."

"Make it *faster*," Ken Woldman ordered.

Elden nodded stiffly.

"And about this in-store TV business," Mrs. Gladstone continued. "I'd like our Chicago store to be part of the test group."

They looked surprised again, but not as surprised as me.

Was she kidding? Our store wasn't on the list.

Ken Woldman said that could be arranged.

Then she took her reading glasses off and looked straight at the camera.

"I will tell you all that we have two choices in this company merger. One is to refuse to look at the success of both of our companies and decide that only one way is best. The other is to understand that two different business cultures can only form a strong partnership when there is respect and appreciation for differences. If we can embrace the best that we both offer, gentlemen, I'd say we have hope for survival. I would advise we either live up to our new advertising slogan, Putting Our Best Foot Forward, or find another one."

Then she demanded a "cooling-off period" where no Gladstone employee would be let go until "every available avenue for unity had been explored."

There was no other business.

The screen went blank.

She closed her eyes. "All right, I got through that without screaming."

"Mrs. Gladstone, why do you want to have that TV thing put in here?"

"I don't want to have it anywhere, Jenna. But if other stores have to take the heat, we'll bloody well take it here, too. I believe in suffering with the troops."

Not me. I've tried that at home.

I was standing on the sales floor wondering where the big screen would go and how it would destroy the store and life as we know it. I didn't have time to wonder long. A mother with a little girl came in. The girl immediately headed toward the children's tree. She looked longingly at the names on the leaves.

Four more customers came in. Normally, I try to connect with the kids; not today. I raced from person to person.

That's when the front door opened again and in walked Tanner Cobb. He was dressed nicely, too, in a shirt and a tie and much less baggy pants.

He smiled at me. "I came to work."

"Well, good . . . I guess," I said back.

He headed toward the children's tree. The little girl was still studying those leaves. He bent down to her height.

"You want to write your name on the leaf?"

"I can't write yet," she told him.

Tanner got a leaf and a crayon. "I'll write it for you."

"It's Anna Elizabeth Mastrianni."

Tanner smiled. "You want me to show you how to write your first name?"

"Okay." She knelt down to watch. The mother was smiling from across the store.

"It starts with a cool letter. The first letter of the alphabet."

"A," she said proudly.

"You got it." Tanner showed her how to draw an A. She drew it, kind of, but took the whole leaf to do it. He looked at me. "I hope you got a lot of leaves."

"I do."

I sold the mother three pairs of summer clearance sandals and Anna learned how to write her name. Gladstone's is a full-service shoe store.

I sold a man five pairs of sneakers. I thought about ringing the bell, but Murray would have killed me.

Three more customers came through the door. I'm good when it's busy, but I couldn't handle them all.

I grabbed Tanner's arm and gave him everything I knew about beginning sales in one desperate breath. "Be yourself. Tell them you're new, don't pretend you know anything you don't. Help people as much as you can and I'll do the rest."

He nodded.

One more tip: "If you mess up, I'll kill you."

Being a big sister is excellent training for management.

He headed toward the prettiest woman in the place. "Can I help you, miss?" He gave her a blinding smile. Mr. Electric. She handed him a blue evening shoe she wanted to try on, and he actually said, "The blue on those beads will look great with your eyes."

That woman melted in a little pool right at his feet.

Mrs. Crenshaw, one of my regulars, was wailing about how her son-in-law wasn't taking care of his family like he should and how she was running after her little granddaughter, trying to help out.

"You're doing what my grandma did for me," I told her. "We couldn't have gotten along without her." I sold her a budget-conscious high-top walker that would give her extra cushioning—perfect for catching granddaughters.

I rang her up. "I wish these shoes would make your son-in-law a better person."

"Jenna, if you ever find shoes like that—"

"I'd buy them all up, ma'am. Believe me."

Tanner was running back and forth bringing shoes as I called out the sizes and the styles.

He was seeing up close and personal how some customers act, too. A gruff guy tossed him a Burger King bag. "Throw this out!" the guy ordered.

Tanner stood tall. "Do I look like a janitor?"

Oh, please, mister, don't say yes. I rushed over, grabbed the bag. Now an older woman was waving at Tanner. "May I speak to your manager, please?"

"She's my manager."

"Not exactly."

Tanner said, "I get my very own 'cause I'm a special case."

I lurched forward. "We're working here to help youth, of which I am a member, find their, I mean *our*, rightful place in the business community."

Tanner smiled. "It's keeping me out of jail."

"He's such a kidder!" I shrieked, but the woman smiled.

"I had a job when I was your age—I sure gave my boss a hard time," she said.

"Yeah?" Tanner laughed. "What'd you do?"

I just let them converse. I waited on five people in ten minutes and sold ten pairs of shoes. I thought of ringing the bell to make the point that *I* was the only one working.

Finally a break.

Tanner wanted to know what good leather felt like—I showed him.

"See how soft it is?"

He felt the shoe inside and out. "Must have been a real chore handling things without me," he said.

I smiled. "We got by."

"I'm not going to . . ." He swallowed hard. "Mess up anymore."

"That's good."

He touched his tie. "You just get so many chances."

Chapter 16

>>>>>>>>>>>>>>>>>>>>>>>>>>>>>>>>>>>>>

Best foot forward, Mrs. Gladstone led the way and Tanner Cobb put his feet exactly where she showed him.

"Let's look at your strengths, Tanner," she announced. "How would you describe them?"

He put his hands in his pockets. "I dunno."

"Mr. Cobb, do you mean to tell me you have walked this earth for sixteen years and you don't know one thing you're good at?"

He shifted. "I was pretty good at stealing."

I'm not sure that's what she was looking for.

"Well, then." Her face was determined. "What, exactly, do you have to know to be good at stealing?"

He looked surprised. "I guess . . . you've got to read a situation, know the patterns in a store, you've got to move quickly, got to think of ways to hide the stuff so you can get out the door." He was seriously thinking now. "And when there'd be a few of us, I was the leader. I had the plan."

"Well, all those *talents* can be used in other ways," she retorted.

"Huh?"

Mrs. Gladstone folded her arms. "Observe customers to get an idea of how people react, understand people's patterns and how to respond to them, move quickly when you're working, be creative in how you get the job done, and use your leadership ability to motivate others. I dare say, you already know how to do that. Businesses are looking for people with just those skills, people who can implement a plan."

"You're kidding." He laughed out loud.

"Oh, we human beings put ourselves in such little boxes. My Lord. Anything can be turned around." She stared right through him. "What else are you good at?"

He smiled. "I'm pretty good with the ladies."

"That takes personality, young man."

"And *attitude*." He leaned back.

"Which you seem to have no shortage of." Mrs. Gladstone stood there like the alpha business female she was. "Tanner, from now on you'll be officially reporting to Jenna, who will be your manager. You will be able to track your performance based on the tasks you complete. She will give you weekly assessments and help you to stay on track. If you have goals you want to pursue here, we'll certainly take those into consideration. I think people do their best jobs when they understand their strengths. And you've got a lot of them. I'm sure Jenna will find more."

She walked off.

I think I just got promoted, but I wasn't sure. Running after her wouldn't have seemed managerial, so I stood tall, sucked in my stomach.

I had no idea what to do next.

"You think of any more of my strengths?" Tanner asked hopefully.

"Well . . . you're good with kids. You taught Webster really well and you helped that little girl learn to write her name."

"I like kids."

"Not everyone who likes kids can teach them. You're a good teacher, Tanner."

He scoffed. "Teachers don't make any money."

"But they get the summer off."

That got him thinking.

It was like a whole new world of possibilities opened up to him.

"If you want to learn about a shoe store," I told him, "read the material that comes in."

So Tanner brought shoe brochures home and the next day he came back saying things like, "Bright colors are here for fall with a brushed tone for men, but that doesn't mean anyone has to give up style or comfort." He looked at me intensely.

We approached goal setting.

"I want to sell shoes," he insisted.

"Okay, that's going to be the goal that you have to work toward. You've got to understand how the store works first. That's what I had to do." I got on the sliding ladder and gave it a push all the way to the end of the row, one-handed. Look, Ma, no net.

Tanner laughed. *"Let me try."*

"You can't do that yet."

"Why not?"

I knew there was an answer, but I wasn't sure what it was. It was just a feeling I had that he wasn't ready for this yet. You can't just walk into a shoe store and expect to do it all immediately. I remembered my mom telling me over and over when I wanted to accomplish a big goal: *You've got to earn the privilege.*

"Because you've got to earn it," I said. Disgust crossed his face.

I walked him to the foot poster. "See, you've got all these bones and muscles in the feet and they all have a part to play in helping us walk. If a shoe doesn't fit right, it affects lots of areas because so many parts of the foot are connected."

Tanner gazed at his feet. "That's a lot of bones."

"Twenty-six bones," I said. "Per foot."

"You have a life other than this?"

Not much of one. "And see"—I took a pair of stiletto heels out—"see how high that heel is? These heels are really bad for women's feet because they stretch that muscle and make the toes do too much of the work."

"My girlfriend wears those."

"Girl*friends*, isn't it?"

"Hey, they come, they go."

Like bad shoe designs. I told him how stiletto heels cause knee and back problems.

He pressed in. "Then how come you sell 'em?"

"Because people want them. I don't think we should sell them. I try to talk people out of them."

"You don't get fired for that?"

"No." I smiled. "Here, we tell the truth."

But as soon as I said it, I wondered if that were really true.

I tore into Mrs. Gladstone's office the first chance I got.

"I'm not sure how to be a manager," I confessed.

"I think you've been doing it, Jenna. You just have the official title now."

I bit my lip. "But *goal setting*. I have trouble with that in my own life."

She smiled. "Setting goals for others is always much easier than setting them for ourselves. That's one of the joys of management."

"But I don't know what he should be concentrating on!"

"Jenna, that young man needs some successes under his belt. So give him short-term projects he can easily accomplish and praise him when he gets them done. Build up his confidence, then later add something that will take him longer to finish. Don't overwhelm him." She got up, walked past me, and headed toward the bathroom.

I guess the only person around here who was allowed to be overwhelmed was me.

Mrs. Gladstone was spending time with Tanner—a little too much time, in my opinion. With everything else going on in the store, with Elden doing who knows what in Dallas, you'd think she'd be busier with the corporate guys.

She was telling Tanner all these stories about the shoe business—even some I'd never heard—like the one about Harry Bender's all-out sales composure.

"Once there was a mouse in the Dallas store," I heard her say. "It ran across the sales floor and stopped right in the middle of the women's section in the middle of the end-of-the-year sale. Ladies were screaming, and Harry raised that voice of his, looked at the mouse, and said, 'You'll have to wait your turn like everybody else.' " She and Tanner had a good laugh over that one.

It didn't make me feel like laughing.

Yaley was coming in daily to check up on Tanner and to tell me how happy he seemed at home these days. Murray was saying how he thought Tanner had the goods to be one of the great salespeople. The whole world was focused on Tanner. Mrs. Gladstone even took him out to lunch. When he came back, he actually said to me, "I put in a good word for you."

It took all my training in an alcoholic home not to tell him off.

Tanner kept asking me what was wrong and I kept lying. "Nothing."

I had to hold myself tight, I had to be strong for everyone. I was trying to be happy that he liked his job and he was doing so much better. I knew he'd crawled out of a dark hole and I wanted to help. I really did. But I felt like I was losing ground.

. . .

"The doughnut guy's here."

I was sitting at my desk, looking through factory reports for Mrs. Gladstone. I tried to make it seem like that wasn't big news.

Tanner said, "So you should go down. Right?"

Casual and distant, I told myself. "Murray's there. Right?"

"The guy asked for you."

"Oh." I got up, walked casually down the stairs, onto the sales floor, and tripped.

Charlie caught me. "Hi," he said.

"Hi."

"I need boots," he added.

"We've got those."

I could feel Murray and Tanner staring at me. I dropped my shoehorn, picked it up.

Charlie Duran looked at the big bell. "What's that for?"

"Dramatic impact," Murray said solemnly.

I showed Charlie the all-around boots. He didn't seem like the Western type.

Mrs. Gladstone had come down and stood at the register, watching, too. Charlie picked up a desert suede boot, an all-leather chukka, a rugged leather pull-up boot with a leather-lined rubber sole. "*Very* good," I told him, "for all-around wear."

"That's what I need."

I measured his feet; went into the back; brought the wrong sizes out.

He tried on six pairs—none of them worked. But then I thought, *Boller, do what you know.*

"Look," I said, "you've got a narrow foot and the styles you're looking at aren't going to feel right. Try this one." I held up a hiking boot—part leather, part fabric, totally waterproof. "They clean up well. You can splash mud on these. You can drop doughnuts on these."

"The ultimate test." He laughed.

He had a good laugh. I was feeling more like myself. "You know a boot's all about sturdiness. And if you've got too much room, you're going to be miserable."

"I try to avoid misery," he said.

I slipped the boots on him, laced them up tight, but not too tight. He could have done that himself, but, okay, I was showing off a little. He walked around in them. "Go up on your toes," I told him.

"It feels good."

I nodded. "They'll move with you, not against you."

He walked back over to me. "You know what you're doing."

"Thanks." Putting my shoehorn in my pocket, I walked him to the register past Mrs. Gladstone, Murray, and Tanner.

I hoped I wasn't blushing. I rang him up at the register. Made a mistake. Had to cancel the charge.

"Doughnuts are easier," he said.

"But they're dangerous."

He laughed. "The chocolate chip ones are menacing."

"Tell me about it. But the raspberry . . ."

"The ultimate danger."

He always had a comeback. I liked that. Finally, the credit

card went through. Murray looked like he might ring the bell. If he did, I'd kill him.

"So," Charlie said.

"So . . . ," I answered.

"I'll see you."

"I hope you like the shoes."

"I already do."

He stood there for a minute, then he left. I would have sighed openly, but *everyone* was looking at me.

I put the receipt bill in the drawer.

"You had the guy," Tanner said to me.

"He seems like quite a nice young man." That was Mrs. Gladstone.

I felt my face flame red. "He's *just* a guy."

Tanner scoffed, "You need to get out more, girl."

"Out with it, Jenna. What do you like about this guy?" Opal dug her chopsticks into the plate of pad thai noodles.

I shifted in my chair. How do you explain chemistry?

"Well . . . he's sure of himself."

Opal nodded. She appreciated confidence.

"He seems to be his own person."

"How?"

"He's just cool about himself and what he does. He likes being a doughnut guy. I like that." I ate a dumpling. "I just want to let things happen or not, you know? Like you and Jacques."

She made a pained noise. Jacques hadn't asked her out yet.

"Maybe you shouldn't be quite so distant," I suggested.

"Look, Jenna. The whole relationship can look totally dead, but you have to be ready. Anytime. Anyplace. It's always when you least expect it."

We were waiting for Elden Gladstone's official word on the redesign of the Rollings Walkers. Mrs. Gladstone was a lot more patient than me. She said that sometimes you have to give people a chance to do the right thing.

She didn't add what we were both thinking: *even if you don't believe they will.*

I was about to have my first meeting with Tanner to see how he was doing with his goals. An "assessment" meeting, Mrs. Gladstone called it. I hoped I wasn't going to mess up. She'd finally taken *me* out to lunch and told me what a good job I was doing.

"I haven't spent much time with you lately," she said, "because you were doing so well on your own. I didn't want to interfere with your momentum."

That made me sit tall.

I leaned forward and asked Tanner the big management question. "*So*, how do you think you're doing?"

Tanner grinned like he was ready to be CEO. "Good."

He sat at the chair near my desk, picked up an Al-Anon book I had lying there. He opened it, leafed through.

"You believe in this stuff?"

This was an assessment meeting about him, not me. "Yeah. I do."

" 'Step Ten,' " he read. " 'Continued to take personal inventory, and when we were wrong, promptly admitted it.' " He closed the book. "What's that mean?"

"Usually, you work the steps from one to twelve."

He smiled. "I take the fast way through."

"Funny," I said, "but there are no Twelve-Step Cliff Notes."

He took out his sheet that I'd made for him. He'd checked off everything for the week—recycling, organizing, reading more of the shoe brochures that we'd discussed. He'd coordinated with Murray about the daily specials and had a system in place to make the shoes easier to find. He'd checked the inventory every day, too.

"That's great, Tanner. You're really helping us."

His face lit up like a little kid's.

"Have you got any questions about anything?"

He held up a plastic Gladstone's shoehorn. "How do you use this?"

I took out my silver shoehorn, the one I got after my first anniversary with Gladstone's. It had my initials on it.

I took off my shoe. "You put the shoehorn under the heel to slide it into the shoe. See? Gently."

He tried it with my foot.

"Gently, Tanner."

"Sorry."

He practiced some more. He practiced on himself.

I said, "I appreciate how hard you work to do things right."

He gave me a soft smile. "I do that?"

"All the time," I assured him.

"Thanks."

He stood up and put the plastic shoehorn in his pocket like it cost a million bucks.

Chapter 17

>>>>>>>>>>>>>>>>>>>>>>>>>>>>>>>>>>>>>

"'Fall comes,'" Webster read haltingly from his book. "'Squirrels find nuts.'"

Mrs. Gladstone patted his hand.

He scrunched up his face and kept reading. "'Winter is coming. How do they know?'"

"Boots go on sale," Murray offered.

I was taking down Harry's memorial. That twenty percent off was not meant for the ages. Soon we'd be putting a few winter boots on special to get people in the store.

I rolled up the THIS ONE'S FOR YOU, HARRY! sign.

That's when Charlie Duran walked into the store in his new boots.

I hadn't seen him in over a week. I tried to appear casual.

Charlie checked his watch. "Look, I'm on break. Sometime do you want to go to a movie . . . ?"

He was asking me out in front of everyone. How awkward was this?

Murray and Mrs. Gladstone looked at me and smiled.

"Sure. Whatever."

Murray coughed and said he had something to do in the back.

Mrs. Gladstone took Webster upstairs to read in her office.

I hugged Harry's sign.

Charlie frowned. "Well, we don't have to go if you don't want to."

"No, it's okay."

"I mean, really, if you'd rather not."

"I'd rather."

"Because believe me, Jenna, the last thing I need—"

"I want to do this, Charlie."

I was going to kill Opal.

I gripped his arm. *"I completely and absolutely want to do this."*

He smiled. "Okay, that makes me feel better."

Scheduling it was another thing. He worked when I didn't and vice versa.

It was the first time it had ever occurred to me that I might be working too hard.

Finally, we found a time—Sunday afternoon.

"I'll see you," he said, and handed me a Doughnut Dollar—*Use Like Cash at Duran's,* it read on the front.

He pushed out the door. He had a very purposeful walk.

I threw my shoehorn in the air and caught it behind my back.

How hot am I?

· · ·

I knocked on the stockroom door. Tanner was bent over a makeshift desk he'd built out of packing crates. He had a library book on it, *How to Sell Anything to Anybody.* He was trying so hard.

I smiled. "Is that a good book?"

"I'm halfway through."

"So sell me something," I said.

He looked around; his face got bright. He sprung up, held out a pen with a chewed-up tip. "Young lady, do you know that this is the hottest thing going?" He held the pen out to me.

I took it, looked it over.

"We do the chewing for you, all you've got to do is just put it in your mouth. We've got blue and black ink and we'll be bringing out red for Christmas."

"How much?" I asked, laughing.

"We've got them on special today. Two for a buck. And that's a steal." He put his leg up on the chair and threw out a killer smile.

"Sold," I said. "I've got another job for you."

I told him that Mrs. Gladstone wanted all the Rollings Walkers put aside in the back room. "We're not going to be selling them right now."

"How come?"

"There might be something wrong with them."

"I know that."

He wasn't supposed to know that.

"What do you mean?"

He got a box of Rollings Walkers, opened it, lifted the shoes out. "Put your hand in there. Feel the label."

I did.

"See how it feels kind of bumpy and some of the glue dried outside it? It's like that on a lot of these new shipments of Rollings shoes, but not on the other ones."

He showed me more Rollings in different sizes where the labels felt wrong.

"How long have you noticed this?"

"A couple weeks. Look here," he said, "on these." He showed me the older stock of oxfords that had smooth and proper labels.

We looked in boxes for an hour. "We'd better tell Mrs. Gladstone," I said.

He pushed me forward. "You go first."

Mrs. Gladstone gripped a Rollings Walker, put her other hand inside, and yanked the label off.

"These labels are not being sewn in at the factory. Somebody's been slapping them on," she said.

I didn't get it. Why would somebody do that?

"Jenna, get me the monthly reports from the Bangor plant."

Our biggest shoe factory was in Bangor, Maine.

Tanner said, "There's a lot of bad stuff passed off in my neighborhood."

Mrs. Gladstone looked up. "I'm sure there is. You've done good work, Tanner. What gave you the idea to check these labels?"

"I see patterns," he said.

"What other patterns do you see?" I asked Tanner this as we were walking to lunch.

"I see them all over. I showed Webster the patterns in words and numbers."

"Really?"

The light changed, we went across. Tanner stopped in the middle and froze.

"Come on," I said.

He stood there. I grabbed his arm; we hurried to the curb.

"What's that about?" I asked.

He waved it off.

"Tell me."

Tanner's voice got low. "In jail, outside in the yard, there was a yellow line, okay? We couldn't cross. I did once." He sighed. "Never again."

"They really did it to you in there, didn't they?"

He tensed. "They kept telling me, the judge said to teach you a lesson. They taught me all right—every time I turned around."

"I'm glad you got out."

"Getting out's one thing." He pointed to his head. "Getting it out of here's another."

I handed Tanner the crab shell on my office desk. I got it when Mom, Faith, and I went to Chesapeake Bay. It took me forever to find it on the beach, too, because I needed one that was intact. I imagined how the crab had crawled out as it outgrew its shell and then grew a larger one.

"That's what I've done in my life. It helps me remember I'm in a much bigger and better place than I ever was before. If you want, Tanner, we can try to get something to help you remember you're not in jail anymore."

"I hear where you're coming from," he said.

The next day, a bone was on my desk. It still had a little meat around the edges.

Tanner peered around the corner. "It's a pork chop bone. It'll dry out." He seemed excited about it.

My mind stretched to embrace the symbolism.

"I knew a guy, Lunar. He did a lot of time. He could sharpen a pork chop bone into a knife. For a long time I'd see a pork chop, I'd think of a weapon. Now I'm just going to think about dinner." He picked up the bone and headed for the stairs.

I gulped. "Why was he called Lunar?"

" 'Cause he only came out at night."

I looked at the employee assessment sheet I had to fill out.

Does the employee show initiative? Is he or she able to follow new directions quickly?

I wrote, *You have no idea.*

On my desk: a pile of papers with a sticky note from Mrs. Gladstone.

Inconsistencies on June report from Bangor plant—
call and find out ASAP.

ASAP meant as soon as possible, which is how we do everything around here.

132

There were two copies of the June report; both contained the same information, except for page four, which Mrs. Gladstone had marked. On the first report, the heading of page four was OVERFLOW. When a shoe factory has orders to make more shoes than it can handle, they pay another plant to make them—that's overflow. But page four of the second report was different—that heading read PLANT 427. In the margin, Mrs. Gladstone had written:

I've never heard of Plant 427. Where is it?

I called the Bangor plant; a sweet secretary named Louise connected me to Norm Lewis, the plant manager.

"Mr. Lewis, I'm Jenna Boller, Mrs. Gladstone's assistant. I'm trying to get some information about Plant 427."

Silence.

"Mr. Lewis?"

"Uh . . . yes . . . ," he said. "What were you asking?"

"About Plant 427, sir."

He coughed.

"We have two reports here from June . . . one mentions overflow on page four and the other page four is titled Plant 427. I'm calling to get some information about that plant for—"

"There is . . . ah . . . no Plant 427."

I looked at the paper in front of me. "But the report I have in front of me says—"

"Oh." He laughed nervously. "That's just a misprint. We have a new typist and she got the first-week jitters. You know how it is."

"But, Mr. Lewis, there are two entirely different page fours from the same report. One shows all the shipping and manufacturing costs from Plant 427 and the other just mentions overflow."

"And what did I just tell you?"

I had to be careful here to not sound mad even though this guy was treating me like I had major brain dysfunction. "Mr. Lewis, I need to know about the two million dollars billed on page four of your report."

"Yep, I got it right here. That goes to overflow. You have that page?"

"Yes, sir. But I've got the other page that says there were five separate deliveries to you from Plant 4—"

"I told you that's a *typo*. This is as easy as life gets. Don't make it tough, now." He sniffed. "You just shred that 427 thing. Better yet, send it back to me. Our new girl needs to see the confusion she's caused by not paying attention. Do we understand each other?"

Not really.

I went into Mrs. Gladstone's office and told her what happened. "Call him back and tell him I want to know where the overflow is being manufactured if there is no Plant 427."

"What if he won't tell me?"

"Overflow has to come from somewhere. Ask him where."

I wrote down what she said. I'd much rather have an official adult make this call. "Mrs. Gladstone, I don't understand enough about these reports. I'm not sure I'm helping."

"This is a good way to learn, Jenna."

But there are some things you just don't feel like learning. I placed my philodendron plant next to the phone—a plant that could grow in insufficient light, a plant that could handle angst and abuse and keep growing. This plant and I had a lot in common.

"Deal with the stress," I said to the plant. "I know you can do it." I dialed the number.

"Lewis."

I tried to sound twenty-five instead of sixteen. "Hi, Mr. Lewis. Jenna Boller calling again."

Air sucked in on the other end. You'd like me if you knew me, Norm, I swear.

"Mrs. Gladstone wanted me to ask you where that overflow is being manufactured."

Hostile silence.

"Mr. Lewis?"

He cleared his throat. "Ah, yes, well . . . let me see now. It's in . . . uh . . ." He sniffed. "We've changed things around. I'll have to put you on hold."

I waited.

Three minutes. Five.

Seven minutes had passed; I was still on hold.

Louise, the secretary, came on the line sounding like a computerized voice. "I'm afraid Mr. Lewis had to leave unexpectedly. He'll try to call you back this week . . ."

What was going on? "Maybe you could help me, Louise. I'm trying to—"

"*Mr. Lewis* will have to help you. I'm sorry." She hung up.

I felt like I was driving into a storm of inconsistencies with the top down.

The official word came down from Dallas on Rollings Walkers with a personal note from Elden:

THE FINE SHOES THAT BUILT MY PARENTS' COMPANY HAVE BEEN SLIGHTLY ALTERED FOR COST, NOT QUALITY. ROLLINGS WALKERS WILL BE EXCLUSIVELY DISCOUNTED FROM NOW UNTIL THE END OF THE YEAR AND SOLD AT TWENTY PERCENT OFF.

The official word in Chicago came down from Mrs. Gladstone. Murray, Tanner, and I sat in her office and heard it loud and clear.

"We won't sell them. I am making that recommendation to every Gladstone's store. Whether they take that advice is up to them, but we will here. Advertising will be running to promote this sale and our customers will be disappointed that we cannot accommodate them. That will make things difficult on the sales floor."

Murray and I looked at each other.

"What they're doing," Mrs. Gladstone explained, "is called harvesting the brand. They're betting that people will continue to buy this brand based on its good reputation. They're lowering the quality, lowering the price, but still making a nice profit. Sooner or later the word will get out and no one will want the shoes. I can't be part of that. I apologize in advance if this makes your jobs more difficult."

Chapter 18

>>>>>>>>>>>>>>>>>>>>>>>>>>>>>>>>>>

War is hell.

I was on the sales floor telling customers that right now we don't have Rollings Walkers.

Are they on back order?

Not exactly.

But you still sell them, right?

Not in this store. Not until things change.

Change hit everywhere.

The closed-circuit TV arrived. It took two technicians to put it up.

Murray couldn't look at it; he said it hurt his eyes.

I looked at it, trying to stare it down. Mrs. Gladstone gazed up at it like David standing tough against Goliath.

There was no ON/OFF button.

"When's that thing going on?" Tanner asked.

Mrs. Gladstone walked away. "When it suits their purpose, I imagine."

● ● ●

Understanding denial has given me a real leg up in the business world.

I faced my phone. Norm Lewis could run, but he couldn't hide. No excuses this time, Norm, or it won't be pretty. You're dealing with an Al-Anon participant highly trained in lie detection and all forms of deceit. I dialed his number again and again until he picked up.

"Hi, it's Jenna Boller calling. Sorry we've had such trouble reaching each other," I said.

He sputtered and coughed and ahemmed and said, well, yes, the outsource people are somewhere in West Virginia. He'd have to get back to me on the rest.

I don't think I'm going to wait for that.

Someone in this company had to have this information.

Think, Boller.

Edna Moran in accounting; she was a good friend of Mrs. Gladstone's. The accounting department in a company keeps all money records. Everything purchased or spent by any department in the company is in their files. Edna Moran knew all.

I dialed her number.

"Hi, it's Jenna from Mrs. Gladstone's office. Mrs. Gladstone was wondering if you could help us contact the outsource people in West Virginia . . ."

"You mean the West Virginia Shoe Manufacturing Company?"

"That's the one." I wrote *West Va Shoe Mfg Co* on my pad—underlined it twice.

"Can you hold, Jenna?"

Being on hold was part of my job.

She was back. "They're a new outsource company for us. All I've got is their phone number—I don't know why we don't have an address. It's 800-555-0033."

I wrote that down. "Thank you, Ms. Moran."

I called the number.

Two rings, then: "Thank you for calling the West Virginia Shoe Manufacturing Company. To send a fax, wait for the tone." Beep . . .

I dialed it again and got the same message.

I faced my computer and silently thanked Mrs. Kletchner, the school media specialist, who had vowed to teach my class how to conduct a proper search on the computer even if it killed her, which it almost did. I typed in *West Virginia Shoe Manufacturing Company*. Pressed ENTER. In a moment, the words:

Search found 0 listings for West Virginia Shoe Manufacturing Company. Please refine your search.

I typed in *West Virginia Shoe Manufacturing Company, West Virginia*.

Search found 0 listings for West Virginia Shoe Manufacturing Company, West Virginia. Please refine your search.

I checked the Yellow Pages on-line; found nothing.

This didn't make sense.

I stood at the business desk of the Chicago Public Library and said to the librarian, "Is there any way that I can check on a company and find out what they do and what their address is?" She smiled. Librarians understand about power—they know how to find anything. I gave her the name of the West Virginia Shoe Manufacturing Company and the 800 number.

She started typing; her eyes watched the computer screen. "How big is the company? Do you know?"

"I don't."

"If they're doing business, we'll have it here." She checked, typed. "Nothing there . . . let me see if they have a business license . . . you're sure this is the right company name?"

"Positive."

She studied her screen. "According to every database that lists companies doing business in America, West Virginia Shoe Manufacturing doesn't exist."

How could that be?

She checked the reverse phone directory. "Okay, we've got something, but they've got a different name." The printer whirred out the information.

TRADE WINDS INTERNATIONAL
PO Box 33299
Grand Cayman
Cayman Islands

"But this isn't even in West Virginia."

"No," she said quietly. "It's not."

I knew the Cayman Islands were in the West Indies, not West Virginia. She was typing again, clicking her mouse. "They've got a website."

She wrote down the web address and handed it to me.

When the going gets tough, the tough get a librarian.

Palm trees blowing in the breeze against a blue sky. The words *Trade Winds International*. One of those websites that tells you absolutely nothing. What could this place have to do with West Virginia Shoe Company?

A few years ago at my school, some kids in the computer lab broke into the school's database and inserted the name of a fictional student, Milo Bentchik. They gave him an address, a social security number, a phone number, and a straight A average. He was active in clubs and sports. They were hoping to put him up for class president, or at the very least valedictorian, but they were found out and did penance for the rest of the year in detention.

It's amazing how you can make something fake seem real.

I called Edna Moran in accounting, who knew nothing about Trade Winds or Plant 427. She said with the merger this summer, the accounting records were being combined with the Shoe Warehouse and right now it was hard to find anything. But being the most helpful woman in America, she faxed me billing and purchasing records for West Virginia Shoe—two years' worth.

My eyes crossed as I looked at dozens of numbers and categories—leather, glue, rubber, cork, cardboard boxes, tissue paper, thread. West Virginia Shoe had ordered a lot of material over the last two years. The last order they placed was just last week.

That's pretty unusual, I'd say, for a company that doesn't exist.

Chapter 19

>>>>>>>>>>>>>>>>>>>>>>>>>>>>>>>>>>>>>

Saturday. High noon. The closed-circuit TV finally came alive.

Hard-driving music played. Images flashed across the screen of shoes and feet. Elden's face broke out before us, bigger than life.

Murray gasped like people do in horror movies when the serial killer shows up.

"Welcome," Elden said, "to the new Gladstone's!"

Customers stopped what they were doing to watch.

"Have we got surprises for you!" Elden exclaimed like a game-show host. "Daily specials, hourly sales." Elden kept talking about the shoes on special and how they were made with quality. He mentioned the Rollings Walkers discounted *everywhere*. "The shoes that built my parents' shoe company," he said proudly.

I tried to tune it out. Elden insisted the great tradition of Gladstone's hadn't been changed, just updated.

I couldn't listen anymore; I went upstairs.

Mrs. Gladstone had left another sticky note on my chair.

Call these suppliers and ask if they ship their orders to West Virginia Shoe.

There was a list of companies that we did business with. It's amazing all the products you need to make a pair of shoes.

I called AAA Rubber Company, U.S. Thread, Buttons Unlimited, Zack's Zipper Company. Not one of them had heard of West Virginia Shoe or Plant 427. They all shipped their material to our plant in Bangor.

Milo Bentchik rides again.

But why?

The end of the day. Murray came upstairs looking happier than I'd seen him in ages.

"In this crazy world, kid, never forget the wisdom of loyal customers."

He held out sheets of paper; on them were scribbled names, phone numbers, and pointed comments:

Who authorized that stupid TV?

What is happening to the store we love?

Stop this madness!

"We should have a decent collection by the end of the week," Murray said. "Madeline wants to get customer comment cards printed up pronto."

"Put some red sneakers on them." I told him Yaley's story about the little boy.

"You know, kid, that gets me right here." He pointed to his heart, not his stomach.

Sunday finally came.

I met Charlie at the doughnut shop. I got the tour, too.

"What I love about it here is these doughnuts make people happy," Charlie told me. "People think every doughnut is alike." He broke a doughnut in half, showed me the inside. "But to be a Duran's, it's got to have substance and texture. And it's got to be big!" He opened his hands. "How can that be junk food?"

He showed me how to roll out the dough. He had strong arms. "Timing's everything with doughnuts—you let them cook a few minutes too long, they get too heavy."

"Have you always worked here?"

"I rebelled against the family business for a while."

"You don't look like a rebel."

He smiled. "I wasn't a real good one. When my great-grandpa died, I got serious about the place. We called him The Doughmeister. I've got a picture of him up here for inspiration." I peered at the black-and-white shot of a tall, skinny old guy who looked a little like Charlie.

There was a sign on the wall:

SAY IT WITH DOUGHNUTS

Charlie put two raspberry creams into a bag and we walked to the theater on Dearborn Street that showed old movies.

145

. . .

The craggy old detective was examining a footprint the murderer left in the garden. "They always leave something," he said to the younger one.

Charlie opened the bag in the darkened theater and handed me half a doughnut.

"You see that insole step?" The old detective pointed to an indention in the footprint.

"Yeah."

"Well, that's made by a right foot slightly turned in at the ankle, which is exactly what Rodney Querlon has when he walks."

Insightful music played.

"So what do we do?" asked the young detective. "Rodney Querlon has disappeared."

The old craggy detective stood up slowly and called in the boys from forensics to sweep the place for clues. "Our man Rodney thinks he got away with murder, and when a man thinks that, you can bet he's going to make another mistake."

We settled in as the mystery unfolded. Gradually the old detective solved the crime and dealt with the mystery of his own life.

"Here we are," he said to his girlfriend at the end, "alone in a city teeming with lonely people. I open my doors to the rich and the poor, the lost and the unlucky. It's not the kind of work I expected to do, Myrna. But this is the work I've chosen."

Myrna took a long drag on her cigarette without coughing.

"Or maybe it chose you, Johnny." She looked meaningfully out the window. "Maybe it chose you."

We walked out of the theater, holding hands.

With the exception of dancing once with a guy in Texas and a few unmemorable blind dates, I haven't held many guys' hands.

I've held a lot of male feet, though.

Not every teenager can say that.

Well . . . ? Opal asked when I called her.

"He understands retail," I said dreamily.

147

Chapter 20

>>>>>>>>>>>>>>>>>>>>>>>>>>>>>>>>>

By the middle of the week, the customer comment cards came from the printer, complete with a little pair of high-top red sneakers in the corner.

GLADSTONE SHOES
Tell us what you think

Did they ever!
Who thought this was a good idea?
The sound is so loud, I can't think!
What an insulting way to treat customers!

Yaley was beaming about the cards. Mrs. Gladstone had asked her to design them.

"I've never been paid as an artist before." Yaley held the check Mrs. Gladstone gave her like she couldn't believe it.

By the end of the week we had forty-four customer comment cards on Gladstone's new look. Comments ranged from "chaotic" to "moronic" with warnings about slipping quality on several brands.

I made copies of them and Mrs. Gladstone mailed them off to Ken Woldman and Elden. She was whistling when she did it. She was getting requests for those cards from other stores who'd had enough.

Her hip was getting worse. Her doctor was getting impatient. "She needs surgery," he told me when I canceled appointment after appointment.

Schoolwork was mounting. I had too much to do.

I was trying to find time to see Charlie.

"You know the problem with human beings?" my grandma used to say to me. "We think we can wear too many hats at once. It's not possible." She'd pile on two or three to make the point. "It's an outright fashion disaster."

We'd laugh and I'd try my best to remember there's just so much a person can do at one time without going crazy.

But I was skating close to crazy.

Even journalism seemed like too much to handle. Mr. Haloran was treating us like real reporters.

Check your sources, he kept saying.

Check your facts.

Assume nothing.

My desk at work was piled high with to-do projects. Merger woes mounted. A sole-less person would have walked away, but I couldn't.

The shoe world was the world I'd chosen, or maybe it had chosen me.

I looked at the June report from our Bangor plant. Looked at the list of suppliers I'd called. There was one I'd missed—Transcon Shipping. I dialed, got Lou at the shipping desk.

"Someone else was just asking about this order," he said. "Right now we're picking up three ocean export containers for West Virginia Shoe through to Long Beach twice a month."

Finally—a connection! I was about to ask him what address he had for West Virginia Shoe, but then . . .

"Lou, did you say *ocean*?"

"Our ships," Lou assured me, "are the best in the business."

"Did you say *ships*?"

He chuckled. "That's what we use to cross the ocean."

What's he talking about? We're an American shoe company that makes shoes in this country.

I sat up straight. "Which ocean might that be, Lou?"

"Well, we take the Pacific and then turn left into the China Sea to Thailand."

"Thailand?" I almost dropped the phone. "You mean the *country?*"

"That's the one."

I tried to clear my mind. "Lou, you're telling me that the West Virginia Shoe Company is in Thailand?"

"It's a crazy world. Your people who pay the tab have us take the merchandise from Thailand to Long Beach, California. You following me?"

"Lou, you're absolutely certain about Thailand?"

"That's our business. We ship from Asia to America every day."

This couldn't be right. Gladstone Shoes are made in America.

My mind was struggling to take this in. "Lou, what happens in Long Beach?"

"You'll have to call Cross Country Trucking. They pick up after your load clears through customs. I don't know where they take it."

I looked in the little mirror on the far wall and saw the QUALITY FIRST sign reflected backward, which is what mirrors do.

꓄Ƨ☓ꓲꟻ ⅄꓄ꟼ∀ꟷꓷꓕ

This would have been a cool clue in a detective story, but it didn't mean beans in a shoe mystery.

I raced downstairs to talk to Murray, who was trying to explain to a customer that he'd called American Express twice and both times they told him her card had expired.

I picked up shoe after shoe from the displays. All the labels promised the same thing:

> **GLADSTONE SHOES**
> ─────────────────
> *Made exclusively in the USA*

Not Thailand.

The woman gave Murray her Visa card. That was refused, too.

Diners Club, MasterCard.

Nope.

"We still take cash," Murray offered.

I raced into Mrs. Gladstone's office, but she was out to lunch.

I had to talk to *somebody*.

Tanner was standing at my desk.

Could I trust him?

"What's wrong?" he asked.

I showed him the computer screen. Told him what I'd found.

"You keeping all this safe someplace?"

"I've got a file."

"It's locked?"

"No."

"Lock it."

I felt a chill go through me.

I told him that the missing piece was what happened to the shoes once they got off the boat in Long Beach. I hadn't called Cross Country Trucking yet.

He handed me the phone. "Call them, but don't ask straight out."

"Will you stay here while I call?"

"Yeah." He stood there like a sentry.

I called Cross Country Trucking and got a guy named Sal on close to the worst day of his life. He had a tractor trailer stuck under an overpass in Nashville. He told me they had another pickup scheduled tomorrow if the weather held in the Pacific.

I asked, "What's your usual route, Sal?"

"We pick up at Long Beach by customs and drive it straight through to the Bangor warehouse."

And no one caught on until now.

GLADSTONE SHOES

Made exclusively in the USA

I felt nauseous.

Tanner sat down when I told him. "You understand you got information a lot of people don't want you to have."

I didn't like the way he said that. "I . . . understand that."

"You understand that people do all kind of things to not get caught."

I gulped. "Well, yeah . . ."

"Keep your head down."

I slumped in my chair. "What do you mean exactly?"

"Anybody outside of us asks, you know nothing."

"Mrs. Gladstone. I think, that is, I know . . . at least I think I know . . ."

"Out with it, Jenna."

I blurted, "Gladstone shoes are being made in Thailand and then shipped to Bangor." I told her what Lou had said.

She looked sadly at the picture of Elden as a laughing child. He'd been a cute little boy. She reached for that photograph. Everything within me told me to shut up, but the truth was stuck in my throat and if I didn't say it, I'd probably choke.

"That's not him anymore, Mrs. Gladstone."

I thought she was going to start yelling.

"It's not him. You've got to have another picture in your mind of him because if you don't, your son is going to keep hurting you."

She put the picture down fast and stared out the window.

I wasn't sure if I should say this next part. "Mrs. Gladstone, sometimes the worst thing you can do for someone you love is look the other way when you know they're doing something really wrong." I told her about my dad driving drunk and how I had to stop him.

She looked at me almost tenderly.

"That's the hard part of finding out the truth, ma'am."

"And how is your relationship with your father now, if I may ask."

I let out a big breath. "We haven't got one right now."

"I'm sorry, dear. You deserve better."

"So do you."

She looked at Elden's little boy face. "He was such a thoughtful child. I don't understand what happened." She turned back to me. "Get me Leona Kyler on the phone in San Diego."

Leona Kyler is one of Mrs. Gladstone's top store managers. Her store is always in the top five in sales year after year.

I got her on the line.

Mrs. Gladstone reached for the phone. "Leona, just how tough are you feeling today?"

Chapter 21

>>>>>>>>>>>>>>>>>>>>>>>>>>>>>>>>>>>>

Leona Kyler was feeling really tough. She marched down to
Long Beach, shoved her Gladstone's security pass around, and
demanded to look inside the shipping crates after they got
through customs for inspection. She said the whole shipment
contained Rollings Walkers with minuscule easy pull-off labels that read MADE IN THAILAND. Those labels got them
through customs, she said, but it was obvious they were yanked
off by the time they got to Maine.

Mrs. Gladstone picked up the crab shell on my desk. "Shells
are interesting creations, Jenna. They can protect, they can
cover." She held it up to the fluorescent light. "Or they can
hide. Have you ever heard of a shell corporation?"

"No."

"Too often they are companies that only exist on paper that
are used to hide illegal financial activity."

The puzzle pieces were coming together.

Plant 427 was in Thailand.

West Virginia Shoe was the cover-up company.

Trade Winds International was nothing but a no-information website.

Mrs. Gladstone whirled into action. "I'm going to need to talk to an attorney, Jenna, one who isn't connected with the company. It appears I'm swimming with at least one shark. They won't be too happy about being discovered."

I figured if I needed a lawyer, she would have mentioned it. The only lawyer I'd ever met did mom's divorce. As for sharks, I'd met enough of them to know that they were always hungry.

The next day, Mrs. Gladstone struggled to speak. "The press has done the investigative work for us with regard to this overseas operation in Thailand. Apparently the conditions in the factory are *deplorable*." She raised her ancient chin high. "We are running, it seems, a full-scale sweatshop."

I took a deep breath. I knew sweatshops were places that hired poor people and made them work too long hours for hardly any money. She held a paper in her hand, put on her glasses, and began to read. "Gladstone Shoes has been found to have engaged in systematic and serious violations of workers' rights in Thailand, including, but not limited to"—she winced—"child labor. The children at the factory were found to be of eleven to fourteen years of age. They are forced to work twelve- to fourteen-hour shifts. They are exposed to gross health and safety infractions. They are fined if they do not meet their production quotas for the day, and the quotas are set unfairly high."

I was having trouble breathing.

"It was found that workers of all ages at this factory were

subjected to verbal abuse and harassment, workers are restricted from using toilet facilities regularly, and those who have complained have been fired or penalized." She shook her head. "God help us." She stopped and collected herself. "There are no pay slips so that people actually know how much they're making, no emergency processes in place, the cafeterias are dirty, the food is unsafe, employees do not have protective equipment when working on the machines, there are heavy chemical fumes and poor ventilation . . ." She threw the paper down. "All in the name of the almighty dollar! Let's save money at the cost of our responsibility to our workers!"

I didn't know what to say. I tried to picture what it was like there and couldn't.

"I thank God this has been discovered. I'm going to do everything I know to make it right for those people!"

Her phone buzzed. *"Yes,"* she said impatiently. "Tell him to wait, Murray. . . . Yes, I know he says it's terribly important." She turned back to me. "An article about this is coming out in tomorrow's *Dallas Herald.* After that, it will be picked up on all the news wires." She pushed her chair away from the desk. "There is no excuse and I will not make one. I should have known what was happening in my own company. I just thank God my husband and father aren't here to witness this."

I didn't say what I was thinking—how Elden probably masterminded this whole thing.

"It's going to be a feeding frenzy for a while with the media, Jenna."

I thought about that one trip Mom, Faith, and I took to

SeaWorld, where we watched the sharks being fed. They'd just swoop in and gobble up the food—bumping into each other, swishing through the water, those big jaws chomping away at lunch.

"Tell me what you want me to do, Mrs. Gladstone."

She raised a bony finger and pointed it at me. "I want you to learn from this. I want you to write it on your heart. I want you to see and understand that businesses who do this *should* and *must* answer to the consequences."

I stood on the sales floor of Gladstone's and looked at the children's tree. All I could think about were eleven-year-old kids working in some Thailand sweatshop making shoes all day, every day of their young lives.

Tanner was heading out. I stopped him.

"There's going to be trouble tomorrow, Tanner. Something big."

He turned around. "I figured it was coming."

"You want to go get a pizza?"

"Yeah."

He headed out the door and started walking down the street.

"I meant *together.*"

"How bad's this thing that's coming?"

I explained about the article in the paper, the accusations, how Gladstone's wasn't about that, but we had to deal with what had been done.

Tanner ate some pizza. "People think they can shove poor people around and they won't get caught. They think kids'll get too scared or be too stupid to turn anyone in. You know what's stronger than fear?"

"No."

"When someone who's been sat on decides they've had enough."

He touched his scar when he said it—it was so long. It curved across his cheek. I didn't mean to stare.

"You want to know how I got it?"

I looked away. "I'm sorry . . ." I studied the deep-dish pizza. "Actually, Tanner, yes. I'd like to know."

"My father was back from jail. He and my mother, they had a fight. He had a knife. He was screaming, telling her he was going to cut her up. I stood between them. I told him no, he wasn't—he'd have to go through me first. He got to me, but not to her."

He tapped the table knife.

I didn't know what to say.

"I was twelve years old. That day I knew I didn't have a father."

Tonight I knew I wasn't a kid anymore.

There was too much happening; I needed to be strong and fully grown-up to handle it.

I felt like unseen evil forces were banding together. I was glad to get in my car, glad to hear the door lock click tight. The air was stuffy, but I didn't want to crack a window.

I drove home looking over my shoulder, but only briefly. I needed to keep my eyes on the road. Every car has a rearview mirror, but if you spend too much time looking there, you'll probably crash. You've got to look ahead to where you're going much more than always checking back from where you came. Driving teaches you a lot about life, although they haven't quite figured out all the applications in Driver's Ed.

I turned right and headed for Michigan Avenue, drove down the Magnificent Mile with the megastores and hotels and expensive restaurants. I could see the old Water Tower lit up in the distance—it looked like a cream-colored castle. It was one of the few things still standing after the Great Chicago Fire.

Seeing the Water Tower made me think about Mrs. Gladstone and how she just keeps standing when the fires of adversity blaze all around her. I wondered if she's afraid of anything in this world.

I headed home on Lake Shore Drive—the big apartment buildings to my left, Lake Michigan to my right.

I parked the car on the street and headed quickly inside. I didn't know how to talk to Mom and Faith about everything, but I had to.

Faith was swirling around in front of the hall mirror. She'd placed a fan on the floor to blow her skirt up as she swished by. I held my skirt down.

"Well," she said, "I had a life-changing experience today." She extended her arm. "I saw Graziella Angelica Antonia!"

"Who's that?"

Faith sighed like I was the biggest test of her life. "Only *the* top model in the entire world. *Only* my ideal. *And* she smiled at me!" Faith tossed her blond hair triumphantly.

"Great . . ."

"You could be a lot more excited for me, Jenna."

Faith posed in the mirror. It was hard to believe we were sisters. She cocked her gorgeous head. "Jenna, is there anyone in this world that *you* want to be like?"

I put down my briefcase, turned off the fan.

"Yeah, there is. She's seventy-three, about nine inches shorter than me, and she needs a new hip."

Faith stood there, stunned to silence.

I brought the *Chicago Tribune* into the house from the lobby. There was no mention of the Gladstone mess. By now all of Dallas, Texas, had woken up to the news.

I had breakfast with Mom and Faith and told them what was going to happen. I didn't eat my oatmeal, didn't want one of Mom's special carrot-zucchini nutrient-packed muffins.

I pulled up the *Dallas Herald* website.

There it was.

TRUSTED DALLAS SHOE FIRM GETS BLACK EYE

Complete with denials:

From Duncan McCall, the Chief Financial Officer: *"We are looking into the matter. Believe me, no one will get away with this."*

From Elden: *"My parents built this company brick by brick. We are shocked and troubled by these allegations. Gladstone's remains a leader in footwear quality."*

"Mom, do I have to go to school today?"

"Yes, you do."

"It will be an *enormous* waste of time."

Mom stood. "Jenna, it's good you take your job so seriously. You're a wonderful employee. What's happened is awful and immoral, but you need to let Mrs. Gladstone handle it."

I slammed my book bag on the table.

"I have to do this in the ER all the time, honey. There are people who need me absolutely and there are those I can just spend so much time with. You've got to think about what's realistic and unrealistic in any crisis."

The pressure of everything was just too much. "Okay, I'm going!" I slammed my dishes in the sink.

Mom shouted, "Don't drive when you're upset!"

"I plan to be upset for a very long time, Mother! If that's the case, I might never be able to drive again!"

Chapter 22

⟫⟫⟫⟫⟫⟫⟫⟫⟫⟫⟫⟫⟫⟫⟫⟫⟫⟫⟫⟫⟫⟫⟫⟫⟫⟫⟫⟫⟫⟫

By the time I got to work, the newscasters had picked up the story and protesters were in front of the store with signs proclaiming, HUMAN RIGHTS FIRST.

They glared at me when I went in. Murray sat in a chair in the empty store; he looked like he'd had his blood drained.

"Get ready, kid. This is just the breeze before the big storm knocks the power lines down."

I ran upstairs to see Mrs. Gladstone. She had a phone to her ear, talking loudly: "You can very well say that, but I'm not going to. I don't give a bloody rip what the company line is supposed to be."

She hung up and looked at me.

I smiled weakly and sat down. "Hi."

"Hi, indeed."

All the phone lines were ringing.

"I want you to know, Jenna, that I'm going to have to take a stand publicly on this, and I don't know what's going to happen."

"Okay." I tried to get comfortable in the chair and couldn't.

"I'm not sure that this company will want me to stay on the board of directors or be part of this organization after I've spoken."

"Wow, Mrs. Gladstone. That's intense."

"This is as intense as business gets, Jenna."

She picked up a report on her desk, *Corporate Response to Thailand.* "This just arrived, courtesy of Elden." She looked at it like it had been sprinkled with poison. "If someone from the media came up to you and asked you what you thought about our company manufacturing shoes in a Thailand sweatshop, what would you say?"

Man . . .

"I'd say that what's happened is wrong and that this company has to do everything we can to make things right for the people in that factory."

"That's a good answer. Would you like to know what Elden is suggesting we say?" She read from the paper: " 'The Shoe Warehouse and Gladstone Shoes are fully investigating these allegations. No one in our company was aware of any human rights violations in any factory at any time. We are proud of our contribution to the shoe industry and will continue to maintain our standard of excellence throughout the world.' "

"Are you going to say that?" But the minute I asked, I knew.

"No, I'm not. They're not going to like at all what I'm going to say."

I wanted to march outside and tell those picketers that there was another side of Gladstone's. But I didn't have to do that. Mrs. Gladstone rose and grabbed her cane.

We walked to the elevator, rode it one flight down in silence. We walked through the back room and onto the sales floor. More protesters were lining up.

An unwelcome presence pushed through the line. Our eyes met briefly—it was similar to the time I'd made eye contact with a king cobra in the Reptile House at Lincoln Park Zoo.

I sensed the rattling of his tail getting louder as Elden Gladstone slithered into the store, walked past me without a nod, marched up to Mrs. Gladstone, and said miserably, "Mother. We need to talk."

"What has happened," she said, "is *unconscionable.*"

He sighed. "We've got a fast cleanup job to do."

Her eyes turned to slits. "Is that what you call this?"

"*No*, I'm just trying to save us a little time and cut to the chase." A protester held up a sign: GLADSTONE'S ABUSES CHILDREN.

Mrs. Gladstone's face crashed in when she saw that. I looked away.

Tanner walked in, his face determined.

Elden shouted, "We need to talk, Mother. Behind closed doors. *Are you coming?*"

Tanner moved instinctively beside Mrs. Gladstone and flexed his muscles.

Mrs. Gladstone smiled at Tanner. "Am I coming, Elden? That's an interesting question. First I want to let this young man know that great trouble is visiting our company and we're going to get to the bottom of it, but until we do, no employee of ours will be asked to work here if they don't feel safe or comfortable."

"My God, Mother." Elden leaned against the wall, snake eyes darting.

Tanner looked around the store, looked back at the protesters. "I'm working," he said.

Mrs. Gladstone smiled. "I appreciate that, Tanner." She turned to Elden. "Now I'm coming."

They walked to the elevator. Tanner and I followed.

Elden stormed into her office.

Mrs. Gladstone told him, "Keep the door open, please."

He slammed the door shut.

A moment later Mrs. Gladstone opened it.

Elden shut it again.

Tanner opened it this time and walked right up to Elden. "The lady says she wants it open."

Elden snorted. *"Back off, kid."*

"I don't think you heard me. *The lady wants the door open. We're going to respect that.*"

Elden took a big step back. "Mother, we *cannot* conduct business with—"

"Tanner and Jenna," Mrs. Gladstone directed, "I'd like you to remove this door immediately. There's a tool kit in the storage room."

Elden was shouting how his mother had gone crazy.

I'd never removed a door before. I bet Tanner hadn't, either. But we smiled like we did this every day.

I got the tool kit.

Tanner grabbed a screwdriver and started unscrewing the bolts. Elden screamed, *"If you take that door off, you're both fired."*

Mrs. Gladstone pounded her cane on the floor. *"Then I'm fired, too!"*

"This is crazy, Mother!"

"This is *my* office and I am introducing an open-door policy in the midst of this crisis. I don't want anyone to feel that we've got anything to hide."

Elden retreated like a snake in the grass.

I wasn't sure if we were fired, but it didn't matter now. I got a screwdriver, too; took the bolts out of the bottom hinge. With two of us working, that door came off quickly.

Mrs. Gladstone sat in her white leather chair as Elden sputtered.

"You know, I think that actually brings more light in here. Don't you, dear?"

If this were a cartoon, steam would be rising from Elden's ears. "Okay, Mother. I'll play your little game. You want the world to hear our strategy? Here it is.

"We had some outsource people go too far in meeting our deadlines and bringing in a profit. We didn't know about Thailand. We didn't ask them every question we should have, clearly, but no one in Gladstone's knew about this. *No one.*

"As a firm, we've taken a hit. But this isn't the end of the world. The average Thai worker isn't working for ten to twelve dollars an hour like here. They make a dollar twenty an hour and they're happy to get it. That's the way of life for those people—they don't know another way. It's not like those kids have a lot of options. This is as good as life gets for them."

Mrs. Gladstone's voice rose. "Well, we're going to show them there's a much better way. We're going to show them that there are people who want to help—"

Tanner was at the door, listening.

"We don't have the money to save Thailand's children, Mother."

"Then we'll start with my salary. I'll work for a dollar a year."

"That's absurd!"

"I'm rich, dear. I don't need more money."

"You can't just stop these things, Mother. Change takes time."

"Well, you see, Elden, we're not going to let those abuses continue. We're going to pay those workers properly—not the dollar twenty per hour, but a fair, living wage. And we're going to prosecute the ones who have been managing them—they aren't going to get a dime. They're breaking the laws of their country and ours. We'll see how quickly things begin to change."

Tanner grinned. "Go, Mrs. G. Go!"

"But we need shoes to sell!" That was Elden shrieking.

"We're going to have to have a few less shoes to sell."

"But the stock will be affected!"

"What a shame."

"But you don't have the authority."

"Don't I?"

Mrs. Gladstone headed out the door—or what once was the door.

Elden shrieked, *"Mother, I am the general manager of this company, and—"*

But she'd already rounded the corner with Tanner, her bodyguard, at her side. I backed toward the stairs, keeping an eye on Elden, who stood there like the emperor in the fairy tale who was wearing absolutely no clothes.

Unlike the kid in the fairly tale, I decided to keep my mouth shut about it.

Mrs. Gladstone took a deep breath. She held her head high and walked through the glass doors with Tanner close behind. She stood in front of those protesters, who raised their signs angrily.

She lifted her hand. It took a while for them to quiet down.

"We apologize to the workers at our factory in Thailand. We apologize to our customers who have trusted us over the years. I don't know who knew about this and who didn't, but I can assure you that the buck stops right here. We will move our best foot forward into every phase of this process. I'm giving every worker, regardless of age, one month off with proper pay and benefits. We will be providing ongoing education funding for those children, and make sure they don't need to work. That's as much as I've been able to figure out right now. But, I promise you, there will be more."

Those protesters looked shocked.

"I'm going to pull every shoe that's come from that factory. We are not going to sell them. We'll donate them to charity. We will not abuse any worker or any customer, ever. I can promise you that."

I felt like applauding. I looked to my right. Tanner was listening like his life depended on it.

Mrs. Gladstone looked straight at those protesters. "I'd like to talk to you about this again after we've been able to make more headway. Can we agree to have breakfast here in, say, a week?"

I went inside the store, where Murray was sitting in a chair, his hands in his lap.

"The queen's back, Murray."

"I hope you're right, kid."

"She's right," Tanner assured him.

Chapter 23

>>>>>>>>>>>>>>>>>>>>>>>>>>>>>>>>>>>>

For a slow-walking elderly person, Mrs. Gladstone sure put the pedal to the metal.

She didn't hide from the press—she made herself available, explaining that things were going to change, and gave a schedule of when they would happen.

The operative word was *fast*.

There wasn't any doubt that she had a true heart. Every time Elden got in front of a reporter, he started sputtering and sweating. After a while, he just copped out with, "No comment."

But Mrs. Gladstone couldn't be silenced. She had truth on her side. No matter what the criticism, she always stood tough. Even when the rumors began circulating from one of those "unnamed sources."

That perhaps she was getting a little senile; she'd been acting strange for a while now.

Maybe that's why she turned over the reins of her company to her son.

And then stories started circulating about how she'd always been such a demanding mother. How poor Elden just never felt affirmed by her. It was like a whispering campaign that happened at school to destroy this girl's reputation. Someone told a lie about her, and then someone repeated it, and with every whisper the lie just grew and grew.

"I'm proud to work here," I said to anyone who asked.

"You got a problem with the old lady," Tanner said, "you come see me."

No one took him up on that.

It's not always easy to say what you feel deep inside, but Mrs. Gladstone's voice was sure and strong. I wondered where her strength came from.

I was driving her home at the end of a long day when I found out.

"You know, Jenna, my father had a sign in his office at the church. It read, 'Woe unto you when all men speak well of you.' When I was a child, I hated that sign. I wanted people to understand and approve of everything I did and to always think well of my father. I told him to take that sign down; it might encourage people to speak badly of him. He laughed and said, 'Madeline Jean, I hope you'll have the kind of life where what you stand for is so important that it makes some people outright hostile. You won't know how strong your beliefs really are until you have to defend them.' I ran out the door praying that would never happen to me. But here I am in the middle of this monumental mess. Floyd and I staked our reputation on quality, honesty, and fairness. I will never take that banner down as long as I live, so help me God."

I turned onto Astor Street, pulled in front of her house. "Mrs. Gladstone, I think what you're doing is amazing. There's a lot of mud being tossed around."

"I don't believe in mud wrestling, Jenna. Only pigs enjoy that."

Webster stood by the tree in the children's section and pointed to the leaves.

"It's fall," he announced, and showed me three red leaves he'd made with the names carefully printed: TANNER, YALEY, and WEBSTER T. COBB.

He put the new leaves on a branch and stepped back, satisfied.

I smiled. "Thanks, Webster. I'll fix the rest."

The leaves had reached their full color in Lincoln Park when the grand jury subpoenaed all of Gladstone's computer records. It didn't take long before Elden Gladstone and Duncan McCall, the Chief Financial Officer, were indicted for fraud and six counts of perjury, which is a fancy word for lying, but it all came down to the fact that they stole and falsified records to cover it up.

Norm Lewis, the Bangor plant manager, was under investigation.

The indictment came down on Halloween, which seemed appropriate. I watched the news on TV; Elden proclaiming his innocence through his lawyer. You don't know who's behind the mask until you force them to take it off.

Elden didn't deserve a mother like her.

"I never much liked Halloween," Mrs. Gladstone said, looking at the bowl of candy by the register.

"Did they have it when you were a kid?"

"Yes, Jenna, Halloween is actually much older than even me."

"I didn't mean it that way."

"I had an Annie Oakley costume with cowboy boots and a little pistol and all this fringe on my vest. I thought I was the toughest thing going."

I laughed; I couldn't picture her in that. "You are the toughest thing going, ma'am. And you don't need a costume to show it."

Ken Woldman appointed Mrs. Gladstone acting general manager—she didn't want the job permanently, but she agreed to take the reins until a suitable replacement was found. I wasn't quite old enough to step into the job, although who knows, someday I might.

It was so good to see Mrs. Gladstone back on the throne. She made the cover of *Business Week,* and the *Wall Street Journal* did a special feature on her called "The Old Buck Stops Here."

I think the trees were declaring that the old season was dying and another one was coming forward.

Charlie sauntered into the store with a new work schedule that had a lot more white space.

"So," Charlie said. "We can go to a movie on Thursday, Saturday, or Monday."

"Wow." I laughed. "Options."

"Pick two," he said. "If you go for all three, there's a special bonus."

"What's the bonus?"

He gave me a kiss right there.

All the rhythms of life were changing.

But Faith had grown so quiet these days.

"What happened?" I asked her finally. "Are you okay?"

Her eyes were red. "I've been crying about Dad. I can't stop. I keep thinking about how he doesn't love us, and . . ." She lowered her head. "Do you cry about it, Jenna?"

What a question. "I don't cry about it that way, but I think about it a lot. I'm trying to understand things more. That way the feelings won't take over."

She started crying again.

"You can come to a meeting with me," I reminded her. She shook her head. "Did Mom say you shouldn't go?"

"No. Mom just said that I didn't have to if I didn't want to because," she could hardly talk, "I was handling everything so well." She buried her head in a pillow, weeping.

"You might want to rethink that, Faith."

She said she would.

But these things take time.

Tanner kept borrowing my Al-Anon book. "I don't know about this stuff, Jenna. I keep having trouble with how we've got to make amends to everyone we can. If I went back to some of those stores—you know, they'd probably have me arrested."

He looked at me like I should have a good answer to that.

There are times when I really wonder if I'm cut out for management.

Mrs. Gladstone was scheduled for surgery and this time, the doctor warned, he was coming to her house to bring her to the hospital himself.

He didn't have to. She had her trusty teenage sidekick.

I walked her right up to her room, too, in case she was thinking of escape. She got prodded and poked till she'd reached her limit.

"I can't imagine I've got any blood left!"

Mrs. Gladstone said this to the nurse who was wrapping a rubber band around her arm.

The nurse smiled. "I'm betting I can find some." Blood squirted into one vial, two. "They'll be coming to take you up to surgery in about an hour."

"That's what someone said an hour ago."

I could attest to this, having been here when the first nurse came in and made the profound mistake of asking Mrs. Gladstone, "And how are we feeling today?"

"I can't speak for anyone else," Mrs. Gladstone had snarled, "but I'm finding this tiresome."

Two nursing assistants had asked if she wanted a sponge bath. She *did not.*

Three separate nurses had asked her if she'd moved her bowels.

"I *have*," she replied. "Have *you?*"

Mrs. Gladstone looked at me. "I hope this is teaching you about quality control."

"At a new level," I assured her.

I knew she got huffy instead of admitting that she was scared or hurt. She just sat there straight and strict, staring out the window, muttering that moving her bowels didn't have a blasted thing to do with her hip. I tried to mention that my mom was a nurse and that bowel moving was a big deal in hospitals. "You could be spitting up blood and half dead, Mrs. Gladstone, but if you can move your bowels, everyone gets encouraged."

She sniffed, unmoved. I'd read somewhere that older people get set in their ways. Based on the available evidence, I'd say that Mrs. Gladstone had fully congealed. She was about to say something blustery to this nurse Beatrice, but Beatrice beat her to it.

"We get behind around here. I know it's frustrating to have to wait. I'm sorry." She gathered up her blood box, smiling, and shared the nurses' secret. "It's always the doctors' fault."

I laughed; Mrs. Gladstone did, too.

It's amazing how one person can change the atmosphere.

Mrs. Gladstone lay back on the pillow. "Never be part of the chaos, Jenna. Always be part of the solution."

Finally an attendant came in pushing a gurney. "Are you ready for me?"

"For quite some time now," she retorted, but this man just grinned.

"I just spoke to your doctor and he's as ready as I've ever seen him."

Mrs. Gladstone smiled. "That's nice to hear"—she checked the man's badge—"Reginald. You know, I almost married a man named Reginald."

Reginald got her on the gurney. "Wasn't he good enough for you?"

"He was a good man, but not as good as the one I got."

"He had himself a fine name, though." Reginald pushed her into the hallway as I followed. "Reginald means 'strong ruler.' "

Mrs. Gladstone beamed. "I think that name fits you like a good shoe."

We walked toward the elevator. I knew there was some risk with this surgery since she was so old. I grabbed her hand. "I'll be waiting right here, Mrs. Gladstone."

"I'd much rather be waiting with you, Jenna." She squeezed my hand and I almost hugged her, but decided against it. Reginald wheeled the gurney into the wide elevator.

"You're about to become a woman of titanium," he announced.

"She already is one," I said.

Chapter 24

>>>

The titanium hip took a little time to get used to, but once she got that walk down, Mrs. Gladstone was trotting through the store like a woman on fire. Ken Woldman had moved with speed to right the wrongs for the people at our plant in Thailand. He'd flown to Thailand and met with their Minister of Labor to show we were serious in working fairly with that country and its people.

Foot on the accelerator, we moved forward.

Tanner was reading up on shoe brands and watching every move I made. He had more questions than a three-year-old at the zoo.

"What's this?" he'd ask, holding up a gel insole that was good for runners who needed more cushioning.

"What's this one best for?" He'd lug out a shiny dress boot for men.

I let him help me sometimes on the floor, and women particularly warmed right up to him. He'd bring out a sling-back pump, smile deep at some female, and say in a breathy voice, "These are going to look great on you."

Women were melting all over the store.

"They used to throw themselves at my feet, too, when I had hair," Murray told Tanner.

And then, one week before Christmas, the box came from Texas. It was addressed to me, but it was really for Tanner.

I found him in the back reading shoe brochures. I slapped the shoehorn in his hand. Every official Gladstone's salesperson got a steel one to start.

"Okay, Tanner, let's sell some shoes."

He held the shoehorn and grinned huge. "For real?"

"Yeah, you're ready."

"I've been ready for a long time."

He straightened his tie, smoothed back his hair, and grinned at himself in the little mirror he had in the back room.

We walked together, striding purposefully, and burst into the light of the sales floor. Tanner headed to the prettiest woman in the place. "Can I help you?" he said with that earthy voice.

She lit up. He had the sale before she'd tried on the shoes. He motioned her to sit down, got the measurer, placed her foot in it; held that foot just a shade too long.

I cleared my throat loudly. He straightened up, got professional, headed in the back for the shoes. I followed him. "No personal foot touching," I whispered.

"Okay, okay." He grinned, jumped up on the ladder, rolled

to the end of the aisle, grabbed the shoes, and pushed his way back again.

I taught him that move.

I was waiting on a woman who looked like she had the world in her pocket—she was trying on all these black pumps and suddenly, she started to cry. I've been trained for all kinds of responses to shoes—surliness, crankiness, meanness—but tears hadn't come up in training, not once.

I knelt down in front of her. "Are they too tight, ma'am?"

She put her hand up, shook her head. She tried to speak, couldn't.

I didn't know whether to stay or go.

"My sister died," she finally said. "We wore the same size shoe. She's going to be buried tomorrow and we didn't have shoes for her . . . you know, for the casket. No one will see her feet, but . . ." She was really crying now.

Boy, this was one for Harry Bender, who would know exactly what to say. I sure didn't. "You must love her a lot to care that much about her shoes," I said.

The woman looked up at me like she was angry.

"I'm sorry, ma'am, I didn't mean . . ."

"I did love her. And we'd always buy shoes together."

"That's a good memory."

She smiled. "You know, she always wanted a pair of red high heels."

I walked over to the display by the front. Picked up a cherry red sling-back with a three-inch heel. "I think I've got it in her size," I said, and went to the back, heart racing. I don't know what it was about this moment, but I felt the power of caring for people so strong. I jumped on the sliding ladder, pushed it toward the eight-and-a-halfs. I took the box down; something told me to get two boxes. I carried them out to her. She sat there with the box on her lap and opened it so slowly. She just lit up when she saw those shoes.

She tried them on, stood there smiling and crying.

"They're perfect," she said. "Have you got another pair . . . for me? I'd like to wear them to the funeral."

I handed her the second box.

She touched my hand.

I watched Tanner rush back and forth on the sales floor. I knew he had the fire and if he fanned it long enough, it would turn into a torch—the thing that lights the way for every true person of sole.

Nobody sets out to sell shoes, really. People aspire to bigger and greater things. But there's something about feet that certain people were born to understand.

Some people say there should be more to life—more money, more prestige. I don't think much about that. I just try to focus in full on the person's two feet in front of me.

"I'm not sure why I came tonight," said the girl seated across from me at the Al-Anon meeting. "I don't know what to say. I'm just having a hard time. I don't think I can talk to a whole group."

Ron, the counselor, nodded to me. I'd been taking new people under my wing these days. I was trying to soar a bit more in my free time, too.

People tried to encourage the girl, but she just closed up.

The meeting ended; she sat there. I went over to her.

"Hi, I'm Jenna."

She looked down. "I'm Chloe."

"You were brave for coming," I told her. "It's not easy to do."

"I didn't say anything."

"There are lots of meetings where I don't say anything."

Chloe looked at her hands. "Stuff at home is . . ." Her voice cracked. "*Nobody* understands, Jenna. . . ."

I sat down next to her and smiled. "I do."

She nodded, trying not to cry.

"Listen," I said, "all kinds of things can turn around."

I looked up at the picture of St. Francis surrounded by peaceful forest animals. That picture used to bother me when I first came here; now it seemed like St. Francis was holding a woodland recovery group.

I pointed to the picture. "Those animals were emotional wrecks before they started coming to meetings."

Chloe laughed through tears.

"It's safe here," I told her. "I can promise you that."